The Roman Spring of Mrs Bennet

By

Ronald McGowan

To the glorious and immortal memory
Of her Gracious Majesty
Queen Elizabeth, the second of that name,
Who passed away on the day I finished this book.
Requiescat in pace.

Table of Contents

Chapter One : Mrs Bennet to Mrs Darcy - Unwelcome News

Longbourn

August 1836

Dear Lizzie,

Oh, Lizzie, Lizzie, you must come home this minute and set everything to rights, for your father is no use and there is no one else I can rely on to save me from that odious Mr Collins and his treacherous wife.

You must come home at once, for your father is dying. He says he is not, but you know quite well that he will do anything to avoid a fuss, and thinks nothing of disobliging me so long as his own comfort is attended to.

But he is dying, he is, I am sure. In fact, I know he is, because Doctor Morland -I suppose I should call him James, now, since the wedding – and that's another thing, the honeymoon couple have not written to me once since they left for foreign parts, and how am I to know that they have not been kidnapped by banditti or murdered in their beds in some inn on the continent? Young people these days have no consideration- anyway, Doctor Morland... James, says that your father will not last another winter, and what am I to do when he is snug in his coffin and I am thrown on the streets by Mr Collins? The Collinses call practically every day. They say it is to ask after your father, but I can see them eyeing everything up and mentally measuring for new curtains and such. You would think they would wait until your poor father is cold in his grave, but, no, they must come prying around. Oh, why could not Mary or Kitty have married him when you would not? For I should not wish you to have missed Mr Darcy and you did quite the right thing waiting for him, but Mary and Kitty are both wasted really, even if they did catch gentlemen of property in the end.

But what am I to do, Lizzie, what am I to do? Your father will do anything to disoblige me, you know, so he is sure to die at the very worst time of winter and leave me destitute in the snow, not but what he is a dear, kind man and the best of husbands and I shall miss him, and how I will ever do without him I cannot tell.

Come, Lizzie, come quick, and rescue

Your grieving mother,

J. Bennet.

Chapter Two : Mr Bennet to Mrs Darcy - Be Not Alarmed

Longbourn

August 1836

My very dear Lizzie,

I know you will be surprised to receive this letter, so surprised that I was tempted to begin it with "be not alarmed, madam," in the style of a certain missive you will remember, but I thought in the end I had better not.

Your surprise is perfectly understandable. After all, it is neither your birthday, nor your husband's nor any of your children's. The anniversary of your marriage was a month ago, and Christmas is still a whole season away. What reason could I conceivably have for putting pen to paper?

What, indeed, save love, affection, and a natural desire to be assured that all is well with the daughter I treasure above all others? That these considerations have never - or, at least, all too seldom - prevailed in the past over my natural indolence and reluctance to give trouble to myself or to anyone else, that they have moved me, not merely to emotion, but to the actual expression of such emotion, must certainly be a surprise.

I could wish that surprise to be a happier one, but the truth - which all the verbiage above has been but an effort to avoid, or at least put off admitting - is that I have been forced to confront the unpleasant fact that I am no longer young, and that I, too, may actually be as mortal as anyone else.

The mere conceit is ridiculous, of course. Every one of us knows in our hearts, whatever our heads may tell us, that we are absolutely indispensable to the universe, which could not possibly have existed before we first experienced it, and could not continue to exist without our continued presence. We remain secure in this knowledge until something happens to make us doubt.

Nevertheless, I cannot deny that I have had a cough for some time now, and that it has not yet gone away. It is a nuisance, but it will not last forever. It will pass, in its own time, to be sure, but it will pass. These things always do. And, after all, what does a little blood signify? Old Doctor Murtherham, whom my father used to swear by, was very fond, I remember, of taking a pint or two of the article from time to time, and used to say that most of us had far too much for our own good.

James Morland begs to differ, however. He chanced to notice the red stains on my handkerchief the other day when we dined there, and nothing would do but that we should go straight into his consulting room, leaving the good beef to get cold, while he thumped and poked my chest and put his ear trumpet against it and stuck all sorts of mysterious devices in divers orifices. All the while "humming" and "ah-ha ing", of course, in approved physician's manner.

He does not like the sound of my chest, he tells me. I cannot precisely blame him for that. Much as I should prefer to do otherwise, I cannot honestly say that I like it myself, much. A physician's dislike, however, has an unfortunate tendency to grow specific, these days. Where old Doctor Murtherham would prescribe blue pill or black draught - in alternation, as far as I could ever make out, and advise bed rest and the daily application of leeches until the patient recovered, young Doctor Morland tells me that I have a congestion of the lungs which, while seemingly tolerable at present, if neglected, he fears might turn into something sufficiently serious to give concern.

I have a great deal of respect for James Morland, and we are grown good enough friends over the years and on our adventures on the Continent for me to take his opinions seriously. There are many fools among the medical profession, but James is not one of them. Goodness knows, he has already gone above and beyond the call of duty in supporting our family, as you will know yourself from our travels in Germany and Italy, not to mention the Archipelago. At the moment it is as good as a comedy to see the lengths to which he will go to avoid letting the dread word 'consumption' pass his lips, but it is no laughing matter to hear his tone of voice when he confesses that he would rather not, for the moment, have to attend me through another English winter like the last one.

So, there it is. We are off on our travels again, your mother and I, long after we ever thought to indulge again in such fancies. Exactly where we are to go has not been decided as yet. Morland thinks Mentone might do, or Nizza, while I rather incline to Naples.

At any rate, your mother must resign herself to at least one short sea trip once more. After that, we are not sure, although you may be certain there will be no arduous Alpine crossings involved this time. James and Margaret are to come with us, again. Lydia offered to come too, and your mother was all for it, but I am happy to say that Wyckham proved his worth again, saving me from a fate far worse than any chest ailment by being unable to do without his beloved wife for the time involved.

I will say no more, then, and ask after Darcy and the children, and all your news, and promise to look up Frank and Mina if we do get as far as Naples and they are still there, and make only the merest, passing mention of how, while Lydia will certainly not be much missed by at least one of her parents, I can think of another of my daughters whose presence would greatly ease the heart of,

Your loving father,

Francis Bennet.

P.S.

Mrs Bennet reminds me that I must be sure to ask how your Leghorns are doing, and inform you that Maria Lucas (I never can remember her married name) has had twins. I dare say they are of one gender or another and are possessed of some sort of names but I refer you to your mother for further details.

Chapter Three : Mrs Darcy to Mrs Morland - Hypochondria

Pemberley

August 1836

Dear Margaret,

I hope that you and James are well, as are all here at Pemberley, and that the foibles and ailments of Longbourn are not taking up too much of your time. I enjoyed '*Southover Priory*' very much, and hope we shall not have to wait quite so long before your next.

While we are mentioning Longbourn, I have just received a rather disturbing letter from my father, and I write to you in the hope of clarification before replying to it. He tells me that James is not happy with the state of his lungs, and almost seems convinced that he must reconcile himself to an invalid's exile among the bath chairs of the *Rivière de Gênes*, or even further afield. I know my own father, and love him dearly, but I also know that he can sometimes be tempted to make the most of any excuse for inaction. I should not exactly call him lazy, for he is not, but he is a devout believer in maintaining the proportion between effort expended and the benefit to be derived from that effort. That he should seriously be contemplating leaving all he knows and taking up residence abroad for an unspecified time, especially at his age, is an indication of how much real concern he feels. There is something, too, about his letter, a note of perfectly unaccustomed melancholy, quite unlike his usual ironical style, that almost frightens me.

We were good friends, you and I, on our trip up the Rhine and over the Alps, and I know that you and your husband have been highly valued by my father for many years now. And, of course, now that my Frank and your sister's Mina are married, you are become family. So I ask you, as a friend, and a sister of sorts, to tell me the unvarnished truth. Do matters stand as seriously with Papa as his letter makes me think? Is his case really so serious, or is he merely making the most of it for the sake of sympathy? Or is he, perhaps, mistaken in his understanding of what Doctor Morland has said to him?

I long to read that there has been some misunderstanding, and that he shall continue to adorn Longbourn for many years yet, but do not for that sake, I beg you, attempt to make light of what may be a serious matter.

I trust entirely in you, dear Margaret. I should write to my mother, in fact, I *must* write to my mother, for she has already written to me, stressing her own alarmed and confused reaction to the news. I fear we both know how useful such a correspondence would be, however. In a perfect world I might write to your husband but in the world that we live in it would be perfectly improper for me to do so, and equally improper for him to divulge to me any information about his patient. Husband and wife, however, are one person, and he may tell you what he could not tell me.

Have you heard from the honeymooners as yet? We have no news here, but, of course, it will be Mina who does all the letter-writing, and we are not in direct touch with Northanger. Any news you may have of them would be a welcome diversion from other problems, and would cheer the heart of

Your loving friend,

Elizabeth Darcy.

Chapter Four : Mrs Morland to Mrs Darcy - On Diagnosis

Meryton

August 1836

Dear Elizabeth,

I perfectly understand your concern, and only wish I could, in conscience, do anything to assuage it.

I break no confidences by saying as much, for, although James takes his Hippocratic oath very seriously, and has only spoken to me in general terms about your father's state, we have both been very concerned for a while about the constant wheezing of Mr Bennet's chest, and the ashen colour of his face.

I have been dropping hints for weeks now that perhaps it might be as well to let James look him over, but you know what men are like.

"Oh, 'tis nothing, a little tickle in the throat, no more."

"Oh, I will get me some Bronchial Balsam from the apothecary. We might as well keep it in the family."

"Oh, it will be better tomorrow."

As a friend, and a sister of sorts, and, I hope, a true example of both, I think we can agree that Mr Bennet has brought the art of procrastination to as fine a pitch as any man, and had he not chanced to cough blood all over our tablecloth last time your parents dined with us, I think he would still be maintaining his robust good health while being measured for his coffin. I make no apologies for using such a strong expression, for it is a measure of the strength of the concern I have been feeling - that we both have been feeling - at our old friend's declining into a shadow of his former self.

Shadows are not something that James is given to starting at, you will agree, but I do believe that he can sometimes be over-protective of his patients, and place my hopes in that. However, his first words to me after seeing your father home and into bed were -

"His condition is serious, but not necessarily mortal. Another winter like the last could alter things, however."

James is looking into the options for wintering on the Mediterranean for your parents. We shall go with them, of course. James really hates to lose a patient, and hates losing a friend even more. His partner can cope with the coughs and aches of Meryton for a while, and we have advertised for an assistant as *locum tenens*.

He tells me to remind you that any diagnosis is, to a certain extent, no more than an informed guess, and that he may be quite mistaken. It is a measure of the regard in which he holds you and your father that he should be so indiscreet with what must be a professional secret. We both trust you to be more discreet in how you use the confidence. I think we neither of us would wish either Mrs Bennet or your sister Lydia to find their faith in the professional omniscience of physicians diminished.

Meanwhile, your mother alternates between making shopping lists for Burano Lace, Marseilles soap, Parma ham and such other trifles and lamenting her imminent turning out of house and home by Mr Collins.

I, of course, merely observe everything, coolly and heartlessly, taking notes and making sketches while murmuring *'quidquid agunt homines...farragost mei libelli,"* which at least gives Mr Bennet the consolation of realising that at any rate something must have rubbed off after all our years of mutual acquaintance.

We have heard nothing from Frank and Mina neither. Nor has my sister Catherine. A honeymoon couple may be forgiven for thinking only of themselves for a while, but, after that while, one does expect some indication that they are still in the land of the living, even if it be only a line upon a view of Vesuvius. I shall make it my business to enquire about them *en route*, and the nearer we get to Italy the more frequent shall those enquiries be.

Whether any further company on our travels would be useful or welcome I leave you to consider, confident that whatever decision you make on that point will be the right one. You must know quite well how much it would be welcomed.

Any further developments you shall know as soon as I do. For the moment, however, our final destination is still as uncertain as the hopes and fears of

Your steadfast friend (and sister of sorts),

Margaret Morland.

Chapter Five : Mrs Darcy to Mr Bennet - Electioneering.

Pemberley

August 1836

Dear Father,

Your letter caused no end of thoughts to spring to my mind. The most optimistic was that Doctor Morland might be mistaken. I will not mention the least optimistic. Both were, however, preferable to those occasioned by the receipt of Mama's letter which she sent me on the same day as yours, and which saw me quite worried.

I have since persuaded myself that either conclusion is quite as unlikely as the other. If Doctor Morland is right, then you are in the best hands possible, and if he is wrong, then there is no cause for concern.

I am persuaded. I wish I could say I am convinced.

All I will say at the moment is: do not set off without me. Let me know your plans and give me time to come down from Derbyshire, and all shall be well, at least if I have any say in the matter. You will have hired nurses, I assume, but hirelings cannot be relied upon, and while I have every faith in the goodwill and good sense of Margaret

Morland she cannot be left to shoulder such responsibility alone. I do not mention Mama, for we both know how useful she will be in a sickroom.

Placed as you are, it seems heartless to dwell on how disgustingly healthy we all find ourselves at Pemberley. I have not seen Jane this fortnight or more, but we shall go over there tomorrow and exchange our latest news for theirs. I am sure she will be perfectly happy to take the children to stay with their cousins while their mother is away.

Poor Fitzwilliam will be abandoned to his own company for a while, for he cannot leave his constituency just now. He has agreed to stand in the bye-election there is to be now Mr Manders has finally been convicted and had to leave the house. Since Mr Peel has seen to it that there is no such thing as a pocket borough any more he finds himself obliged to go about the country making the voters like him. How congenial he finds this task I leave it to yourself to determine. Until all the votes are in, however, his life is not his own, and it will not be until after the election that he will have leisure to neglect his parliamentary duties like all his fellows and join us.

Have you heard anything from Frank and Mina? It is a month now since we had a note from Marseilles, whence they were about to take ship for Leghorn, in a steamer. How things have progressed since we last crossed the channel! Even the Neapolitans have steam boats now, it seems. I should have been happier to learn a little less about their means of transport and rather more about their own state, but one cannot have everything.

I will not exhort you to wrap up, avoid drafts, wear your comforter etc.etc., for I am sure you are already plagued with quite enough of that sort of thing.

I will beg you never to forget, however, that you are always in the thoughts of

Your anxious and loving daughter,

Elizabeth.

Chapter Six : Mrs Darcy to Mrs Bennet – Making Haste

Longbourn
September 1836

Dearest Mama,

You must have been terribly worried when you wrote to me. I was reminded of the seventieth psalm, 'O Lord, make haste to help me.'

I was terribly worried myself, too, at first, but hot on the heels of your own letter came one from Papa which, I think, gave proof that at least he is not quite at death's door and still capable of coherent and eloquent writing. I have also heard from other sources that suggest it may not be time quite yet to be ordering mourning clothes.

I know you must long to have all your daughters about you at this time of trouble. I have written to Jane and spoken to Kitty, who goes to Mary's next week and will pass on the word.

Fitzwilliam sends his best wishes, but insists he cannot do without me just at the moment. You know that he is standing in the bye-election at Lambton, and he thinks his chances will be improved with me at his side. You and I both know what nonsense that is, but we also know how difficult it is to refuse Mr Darcy anything. Even Papa admitted as much on a certain occasion I think we all recollect.

Nevertheless, say the word and I shall be on the next London Mail, and Fitzwilliam may further his own cause, and join the 'parcel of rogues' in Westminster without my assistance.

I have an idea, however, which might prove better than that, but I will say no more of it for now until I am assured it will work.

Until then, be sure that you are never far from the thoughts of

Your loving daughter,

Elizabeth

Chapter Seven : Mr Bennet to Mrs Darcy –
A Generous Heart

Longbourn

September 1836

Dear Lizzie,

Your letter brought me comfort and consternation in roughly equal proportions.

Your offer to come into exile with me is just what I should have expected from your generous heart, and the one thing in all the world that would have given me the greatest pleasure. I dearly wish I could take advantage of it, but, of course, in the circumstances, that is out of the question.

I cannot think why Darcy should wish to be associated with such a collection of rascals as are to be found on the benches of the Palace of Westminster, but if he has taken such a notion into his head, then your place must be beside him. It will look particularly singular if the Lady of Pemberley is not there to support her husband in his canvassing, and his attempts to 'make the voters like him', and her absence would probably be fatal to his cause.

Darcy is a very good fellow, the best in the world, but even you must agree that his efforts to make himself liked are not always immediately successful, or even detectable.

I shall do very well with the Morlands to run after me, assisted by *Signora Qualcosa or Madame Untel* or whoever. James Morland is like to be the best physician in the country if not in the world, and, if I may not have my beloved Lizzie to amuse me, Margaret Morland is the next best thing.

What is more, I can be sure that she will keep you well in the know about all our doings, and save me the bother of writing too often.

I shall write, of course, just as I shall continue my researches and finally complete my great work and receive a peerage and a pension for my efforts. Your mention of the honeymooners taking ship from Marseilles to Leghorn has put me in mind of Florence, and the Laurentian Library, and, now I come to think of it, Rome and the Vatican Library will not be that much further on.

I must disabuse Morland of his idea of the Genoese Riviera. Surely it will be warmer and more agreeable further south? I already have a contact in Naples, of course, but who do I know who could give me introductions in Florence and Rome?

Forgive me, my dear, you have set me thinking of something apart from my wheezing chest, which cannot help but be a good thing.

We have heard nothing from the delinquent honeymooners either. As soon as we do, you shall know.

You must also know that, although the tedious manual labour of setting pen to paper may sometimes prove excessively daunting, you are never absent from the thoughts of

Your proud father,

F. Bennet

Chapter Eight : Mrs Bingley to Mr Bennet - A change of plan.

Garthdale

September 1836

Dearest Papa,

I will not begin by asking how you are, for Lizzie has just left me, and you may be sure what was the subject of the chief of our conversation.

I have the highest regard for Doctor Morland, and Margaret is the sweetest and cleverest of creatures, and I am sure you could not be in better hands, but at times like this you need your family around you. Lizzie tells me you have forbidden her attendance, although she was quite on the point of giving orders for packing, so you must be content - I will not say with second best, for I know you would deny it - but with an acceptable substitute.

I make no mention of Mary, you see, and have said nothing to her. You will tell her yourself what you wish her to know. I have said something of our plans to Kitty, but in her condition she cannot be expected to come. Let us hope we are all safely home for her lying in.

I know you will protest and prevaricate, and find reasons to do without me, but I tell you now,

Chapter Nine : Mr Bennet to Mrs Bingley - Respect

Longbourn

September 1836

Dear Mrs Bingley,

Who are you, and what have you done with my daughter, Jane?

You are so kind that you must be her, but so firm and so practical that you cannot possibly be. All those years of wuthering in the frozen north have tempered you, I fear.

I once said of Darcy that "he was the kind of man to whom I should never dare refuse anything, which he condescended to ask'. Now I see that it is my own dear Jane whose every word must be obeyed.

You are quite right my dear. Left to myself I will be sure to put off decisions. There is always more research that can be done, you know. And unless something is done soon, I run the risk of James Morland carrying every one of us off to some lazaretto on a desert island where we must all eat lotuses until the dreadful day of judgement – or some other dreadful day, if that should come sooner.

Madam's commands will be followed, you may rest assured. We shall see you on the 20th, without fail, and expect to have the tickets for our passage handed to us on your arrival.

Those pieces of paper will not be needed, however, for the sight of your shining face will be sure to cure all the ills that beset

Your obedient father,

F. Bennet

P.S.

I hereby solemnly swear, promise and affirm that Mama will not be allowed to bring too many clothes. You must know full well how much difference such a pledge will make.

Chapter Ten : The Earl of Pennworth to Mr Bennet - Introductions

Hapworth House

September 1836

My dear Bennet,

My sister Margaret tells me you are off on your travels again, and expect to be in Italy for the winter, possibly in Florence or Rome.

She has also told me why you are going abroad, and your reasons for choosing those two destinations. You will forgive me if I say that I should not personally recommend either city to an invalid looking for a warm winter climate. In summer they rival the inferno, it is true, but in winter, with the winds sweeping down from the Alps and the Italian insistence on building great, draughty palaces with no real means of heating, both places can be quite as cold as London. If it is warmth and winter sunshine you seek, you would do better further south, or even further north on a south-facing coast, such as Nizza or Mentone, or even Genoa itself. It is true, however, that you will not die of boredom in Florence or Rome, while that might be an ever-present danger elsewhere, especially in the first two.

You are already familiar with Naples and have friends there. Would there not be enough to satisfy your scholarly instincts in Pozzuoli, say, or Pompeii?

I must not presume to direct you, however, and, in case you should decide to spend some time in Tuscany or the Romagna, I enclose notes to two old friends who might be able to help you. Use them or lose them as you think fit. I also append a list of inns I have found tolerable in the past, although, if you wish to spend any length of time in a particular place, you would do well to consider renting an apartment.

I have the warmest recollections of our preparations for your trip to the Levant, and of the stories you brought back from there, and I have read Captain Price's account of the tale you so carefully did not tell, and I look forward with the fondest anticipation to welcoming you back, restored to health, and with a new budget of anecdotes to relate.

Until then, be sure that you are ever in the thoughts of

Your affectionate friend,

Pennworth.

P.S. Do you, perchance, have any news of our respective niece and grandson? I have reason to believe that they were well when they crossed the Arno, but somewhere between there and Rome they seem to have evaded even my network of informants. I take it they both know how to write?

Chapter Eleven : Mr Bennet to Lord Pennworth - Intimations of Mortality

Longbourn

September 1836

My Lord Earl,

It was very good of you to provide yet more introductions to Italian dignitaries for yet another fool's errand. You may be sure that I will make as much use of them as I can.

I wish that I could be sure, or even confident, of being spared to satisfy your lordship's anticipations, but I fear that age and infirmity have made me a very different man from when we last met, even though that was only a few months ago at the wedding. I should never have thought that constant pain and weakness would make such a change in both my constitution and my temperament, but it appears that I may trust in neither any more. I shall do my best, however.

Mrs Bennet sends her best compliments, and trusts that yourself and her Ladyship are both in health. I fear that neither of us can shed any light on the doings of our truants, however. Even the groom's parents, when last I heard from them, which was but a week ago, were still completely in the dark. As for the new Mrs Darcy's parents, you must be assumed to know more than I.

I can vouch for young Frank's acquisition of the basic skills of literacy. I believe Mrs Bennet still has the first letter he ever wrote, addressed to 'Deer Grammammamma', and full of spelling mistakes, blots, and crossings out. It is true that he has never shown any great inclination towards correspondence, however. At university he might be incommunicado from one term's end to the next.

I would say that no news is probably good news, nonetheless, for they would be sure to write post-haste if they were to run out of money.

If we come upon them in our travels - and we shall certainly do our best to do so - then we shall have a bulletin to publish for all.

Until then, you may be sure that the quest will ever be in the mind of

Your grateful friend,

F Bennet.

Chapter Twelve : Mrs Bingley to Mrs Darcy - Soave sia il vento

Hanover Square

September 1836

Dear Lizzie,

Well, here we all are, gathered in Hanover Square, on the eve of setting off on the great adventure.

Charles and I are very much conscious of being the novices of the party, having never set foot overseas before, unless we count the boat trip to Fingal's Cave. To be honest, I would rather not count that, for there can be such a thing as too much excitement, and now I think back to it, I seriously wonder whether the delicious relief of setting foot on shore again was worth the seemingly endless terror that preceded it.

Of course, the war was on at the time, and there could be no question of the Grand Tour of the Continent. This younger generation can have no conceit of how lucky they are.

But, in all seriousness, how I wish you were here, Lizzie, to hold my hand as we cross the Channel. The seasoned travellers treat it as nothing, except for Mama, of course, who would have us believe that this is like to be our last night on Earth.

Tomorrow we go across town to the docks, to take ship to Folkestone and hence to Calais. We need not pray for a favourable wind, for it shall be steam all the way.

I cannot help but think this independence of the weather at least a little unnatural. Who would have thought it when we were young?

Papa is all for it, of course, but you know what he is like about steam engines. The other gentlemen are scarcely less enthusiastic, and I suppose it is a great convenience compared to waiting for days for the wind to be in the right quarter.

Margaret will only tell me that it will be very smelly and dirty, and not to wear anything white for it will never be the same. She advises me to stay on deck if the weather permits and to keep near the rail at the side of the deck. She will not say why, but only that 'I will know why when the time comes,' which is not very encouraging. It is all meant friendly, I am sure, and I am the novice, so I must be content to be practised upon.

But how I wish you were here!

I believe I have already said that, so I must take care not to say it again. Indeed, I must wish you well in your canvassing, is that the word? Poor Lizzie, having to go about the towns of Derbyshire, explaining to all and sundry that Darcy is not nearly so forbidding, really, when you get to know him.

Compared to that, why should I bemoan the lot of

Your trepid sister,

Jane.

Chapter Thirteen : Mr Bennet to Mrs Darcy : Travelling

Marseilles

30 September 1836

My dear Lizzie,

Well, we have reached the Mediterranean at last, and I must say the warm weather and sunshine of the last few days have almost convinced me that it might, after all, be worth devoting a little effort towards going on living.

I will need a power of convincing, let me tell you, after the journey we have just had, creaking and bumping across France in the French idea of what constitutes a comfortable coach. However, I will say no more about it.

We should have avoided French roads as much as possible, and taken the route that Pennworth advised, down the Canal du Midi as far as Cette, but, really, in all conscience, we could not deny Jane and Bingley their view of Paris. Parisian inns have not improved, much, since my grandfather's day, but the inconveniences and discomforts were almost worth it to see how deliciously they shuddered at the site of the guillotine.

I remember attending the levee, *sous l'Ancien Regime*, and dancing with *l'Autrichienne* at the Petit

Trianon, but there is none of that sort of thing to be had nowadays. Philippe Egalité has learned his lesson, and is not nearly so egalitarian.

Nothing else would do but that they must go to see the Mona Lisa, which, if nothing else, must prepare us for Italy, I suppose. I cannot say I care, much, for Leonardo's simpering housewife, nor can I believe the landscape in the background to be anything other than a work of the imagination.

We were, at least, lucky in the weather, and it was pleasant to sit in the Luxembourg and watch the world go by. Or stop, as the case may be, but I fear the days when I might even have considered responding to the repeated *'tu viens, Cherie?'* of the passers -by are long, long past.

I had a few good snoozes in the Luxembourg, as it happened. I seem to sleep more during the day these days than I do at night. It must have been very boring for Morland, who was my designated nursemaid for the day, but at least he did not have to listen to my peevish moans.

I will not insult my Lizzie's intelligence by assuming she does not already know how the ladies were occupied. It was Paris, after all. I cannot say that I care much for *la mode de Paris d'aujourdhui*. When I was young the Paris fashions were all *à l'antique*, based on a Grecian simplicity, and all the better for it. A simple gown of tulle or muslin could be transformed by the addition of a ribbon, or a piece of lace, and flattered a young girl's figure without turning it into something it was not. Today's fashions, all hung about with frills and furbelows and buttons and bows, tight-laced almost to extinction and seemingly defying gravity seem to me designed to squeeze every wearer into the same hour-glass shape, while dazzling the eye with more colours than it can comfortably contemplate.

A mere man's opinion counts for nothing, I know, but I do not think either of us would have exchanged our bench in the gardens with Bingley, whose presence on the expedition was as necessary for propriety as for payment.

I promised to let other pens dwell on pain and misery, so I will say no more about the journey from Paris other than to observe that there are already sufficient miles of railway track in England to have taken us from Paris to Marseilles in a quarter of the time and twice the comfort.

Did Darcy take my advice and buy those railway shares, by the way? But, I forget, he has other things on his mind just now. And I always thought him so level-headed, so far above that sort of thing! Still, I suppose we must all try to leave some kind of mark behind us.

If Frank and Mina have left any marks behind them, we have certainly not found them, as yet. We have three days to wait for the Neapolitan steamer to take us on to Genoa and Leghorn, however, and shall see what the British Consul can do for us tomorrow. The post for London leaves tonight, so I fear I must beg your indulgence for the delay in any further news from

Your devoted father,

F. Bennet.

Chapter Fourteen : Mrs Bennet to Lady Wyckham - Abroad

> Marseilles
>
> 30 September 1836

Darling Lydia,

How can I tell you how much fun it has been so far on our trip?

The last time we were in Paris I was not quite the thing, and we shamefully neglected to take advantage of the opportunities it offered. I was quite determined to make up for it this time, however, for I dare say I shall never have another chance.

The shops here are quite different from Bond Street. It is quite difficult to get anyone to serve you, and not just because no-one speaks English. The shopgirls seem to go out of their way to ignore customers, especially those who are not Parisian. How they know this is a mystery, for I swear we had not exchanged two words in the first shop we entered, before the shopgirl turned away from us with her nose in the air.

How I should have got on without Margaret Morland I do not know, for your sister Jane has gone all staid and solemn, refusing to leave your father 'unattended in his illness'. When she has been married as long as I have she will know better than to fuss about every imaginary ailment of Mr Bingley's. I am sure.

The fashions are very interesting. The good news is that the *gigot* sleeve is exploded at last. I never liked them. Keeping them in shape was so much trouble, and wearing them such a business, with their sleeve supporters underneath with all those nasty wires. Sleeves, in fact, have almost disappeared for evening wear, with necklines so low and sleeves so far over the shoulder that I cannot see what holds them up. Margaret says you have to wear a special corset underneath to support them. So it seems that we have got rid of sleeve supporters only to have bodice supporters instead.

Bodices *à la Sevigné*, are still in, by the way, so we need not do too many alterations. For evening the smart wear is the open robe, which may need alterations if you go in for it, my dear. It would be too complicated to attempt to describe it, so I will just copy out what it says on the receipt for the one I have ordered for tomorrow's ball.

"Evening dress – Petticoat of India muslin, trimmed with a single flounce, embroidered round the border and surmounted with embroidery. Open robe of the same material, low corsage, square behind, and descending in the demi-coeur style in front; drawn in with a little fulness round the waist, bordered by two folds through which pale pink ribbon is run; the space between the folds embroidered in a lace pattern. The same trimming to the front of the dress and round the border."

What a shame you are not here, my darling, to see me in it! And I am sure you would look so well on the floor of a Parisian Ballroom. I shall never forgive Wyckham for preventing you from coming with us.

Marseilles is very dirty and smelly compared to Paris, even, and that was quite dirty and smelly enough. It is not nearly so elegant, neither, nor so interesting, although your father does go on about his beloved Romans − or was it Greeks? I can never tell the difference. We shall not be here long enough, however, for him to drag me round another pile of ruins. He always seems to find the strength to rise from his sickbed for that sort of thing, but never for anything nice, like a party or a ball.

We set sail for Italy first thing tomorrow. I dare say ruins will be inevitable when we get to Rome itself, but I have hopes of avoiding them in Florence, where I believe there are many English people in residence, including numbers of poets and artists. It is too late to hope to meet the famous Lord Byron, but who knows?

How I wish you were here with me! I never have a good, comfortable chat with anyone these days.

However, *nil desperandum*. See! I can quote Latin, too. Perhaps I will meet a poet in Florence who is also longing for a comfortable coze.

My compliments to Sir George, and kisses for all the children from their loving aunt and

Your adoring mother,

Jane Bennet.

Chapter Fifteen : Mrs Bingley to Mrs Darcy Florence

Mrs Bingley to Mrs Darcy

Florence

7th October 1836

My dear Lizzie,

Here we are at Florence at last, where we are staying at the *Albergo Dello Scudo di Francia*, as recommended by Lord Penworth. We are but just arrived, so I cannot say much about the city as yet, but the inn is clean enough, and conveniently situated, they tell me. We have not gone exploring as yet, but across the square outside the inn there is a street at the end of which one can see the corner of the *Palazzo Vecchio*, which is very tempting.

Alas! I must leave you now, for Mama has lost something - I know not what as yet - among her bits and bobs, and nothing else will do but I must find it for her. I will continue this in the morning.

Next Morning

I was woken by the sound of bells echoing on all sides, and it not even a Sunday. Looking out of the window, I saw a procession winding down the street with some sort of graven image being carried at its head. Charles declined to be roused from his sleep to view this entertainment, so I was reduced to calling for Arianna for enlightenment.

She mentioned the name of some saint I had never heard of, whose feast it happens to be, but could provide no more in the way of illumination.

"I know no more of these popish saints than you do, Kyria Bingley," she replied, with a toss of her head. "I will ask the chambermaid if you wish."

Arianna speaks Italian like a native, of course – a native of the Venetian colony of Corfu, that is – and has already been invaluable in our dealings with the inn servants, who appear not to understand their own language. She will have nothing to do with Catholics, however, if she can help it, and still blames them for the fall of Constantinople. Fortunately, she considers the church of England to be an ally against the Papists, and treats us all as if members of some sort of Greek Orthodox sect.

Breakfast here was rather more substantial than in France, although it feels rather strange to be eating cake so early in the morning. There were also scrambled eggs, proof enough that they are used to English tourists.

Papa was wheezing a little at breakfast, but ate as heartily as the rest of us, and is as eager as might be expected to be out and about.

Our first call must be to Mr Arbuthnot, the British Consul. I expect he will be able to introduce us to everyone worth knowing, and give us some advice about guides and such. I shall give this letter to him to forward in his next bag, which is as good an excuse as any to end now, and send you all good wishes from

Your loving sister,

Jane Bingley.

Chapter Sixteen: Mr Bennet to Lord Pennworth, Florentine Nobility

Florence
14 September 1836

My lord Earl,

I fear the news I must pass on to you about your correspondent in Florence may not be very grateful to your ears.

I called at the *Palazzo Cosadetti* on the second day after our arrival in this city. It is not so very far from the inn which you recommended, and the exercise involved in walking there was highly advocated by my physician, Doctor Morland, who is known to your lordship.

In that respect, my labour was not in vain. My reception at the Palazzo, however, was not as I had hoped, nor, as I believe, what your lordship may have expected.

On giving in my name and asking for the Prince I received a babble of Italian in reply. This was no more than I had expected, and, fortunately, the Tuscan dialect is much more comprehensible than that of the Venetians or the Neapolitans, and I was able to make out that '*Il Signor Principe sta fuera*,' 'My lord Prince is not at home.'

Fortunately, my Italian has not entirely deserted me since my days on Lake Como, and I made sure to mention Your Lordship's name, and that I was the bearer of an important letter addressed to the Prince of Burlano. These powerful shibboleths at least sufficed to procure me shelter from the sun, although I must still stand in a bare anteroom while the doorman bore my talisman to the *piano nobile* in search of orders.

The passage of time – or, rather, the perception of the passage of time – is notoriously lengthened for one who waits, and I dare say that it was no more than twenty minutes or so before the doorman returned. I regret I cannot give a more exact account of the time, as I had left my watch behind, Mrs Bennet having objected to the unsightly bulge it made in the pocket of my best waistcoat, and insisted that I could not appear before royalty 'looking such a fright.'

I reminded her that an Italian prince is not quite the same as an English one, as witness our old friend Filippo de Qualcheparte in Naples, but she knew better, as your Lordship, being an old married man, will appreciate.

I amused myself meanwhile by explaining to myself the murals with which the walls were adorned. They all, without exception, appeared to relate to episodes in the history of the Cosadetti family. Since it was now several centuries since that family had been serious rivals to the Medici, it will be appreciated that they were all of a certain venerability. Chief among them was a great family tree containing among its branches several surprising connections, including Leonardo's Mona Lisa.

I was roused from my contemplation of this fascinating work by the re-entry of the servant, with the welcome news that *"La Signora Principessa vi vedra ora."*

My Italian is not so rusty that the use of the second person plural was lost on me, but I resolved to hear what the scoundrel's mistress had to say to me before choosing to resent the insult. I fear I was not in the best of moods, however, when I was shown into a salon where a rather buxom young lady in a very low-cut gown lay reclining on a chaise-longue in an attitude, or so it seemed to me, exquisitely calculated to emphasize her long, auburn tresses, her ample bosom and her more than ample *déhanchement*.

Upon my entry she neither rose to greet me nor offered me a seat, but merely looked me slowly up and down while flaring her nose as if there was a bad smell in the room.

There was, in fact, a strange smell in the room, not unlike incense, but at the same time very different. It was somehow familiar, but I could not, at the moment, recall where I had encountered it before.

Her eyes having reached the floor, they slowly rose again to meet mine before her lips deigned to open, and she addressed me in a languid, husky voice.

"I am Maria Maddalena Constanza Beatrice Tornara dei Cosadetti, Principessa di Burlano e Duchessa di Nezzuno. Who are you?"

I could see your Lordship's letter, lying open on the little table at the Princess' elbow.

"Mi chiamo..." I began, only to be interrupted instantly.

"Trouble me not viz your barbarous attempts at a civilised language, Signor. As you see, I spik ze Eengleesh perfect."

I had to cough before I could reply coherently.

"Quite so. And may I complement your Serene Highness on your facility with my own tongue?"

"Most Excellent Highness, not Serene Highness. My husband the prince has not been serene for many years now."

"Many years," she repeated, with a little snigger, as if at some private joke.

"Your pardon, Most Excellent Highness. I am Francis Bennet, Esquire, of Longbourn. You have my letter of introduction from my lord Earl of Pennworth to his Most Excellent Highness your husband at your side, there."

She half closed her eyes, as if in remembrance.

"Ah! Si!" she said after a moment. "Ze curious Conte di Pennvort, ze old friend of my husband. He must be ze only friend of my husband, now. Well, Signor Francis Bennet, Esquire, of Longbourn, vatever zat ees, my husband the *Principe* is not here. He comes no more to *Firenze*, he is never seen in ze city. It does not suit him to be seen in ze city, it does not suit *i Tedeschi* that he should be seen in the city. He can be of no service to you, and neizer can I."

She turned her head, and waved me away, as of no further interest. I was in the act of bowing to take my leave when a side door opened and a muscular young man entered, clad, as far as I could see, only in a thin, silk robe, carrying a distinctively shaped short pipe, which instantly sparked my recollection of where I had encountered the elusive smell before.

"Beata Beatrice mia," he began *"Mi scusi, mia vita, Ci è voluto più tempo di quanto pensassi per preparare il prossimo..."*[1]

At this point he became aware of my presence, and faltered in his excuses.

"Solo un attimo, Tonio caro," said the Princess, *"Lasciami sbarazzare di questo ominino noioso, carino."*[2]

My Italian may not be of the best, but I think I may still rely upon my memory, and I repeated the words afterwards to Arianna for confirmation of their meaning.

At any rate, I waxed eloquent upon the spot.

"Questo ominino noioso lo prenderà come permesso di Vostra Altezza per partire. Le auguro buona giornata, Madama."[3]

Dante might have phrased it differently, perhaps, but it sufficed to take me away from the

---

[1] My blessed Beatrice, forgive me, my dear. It took more time than I thought to prepare the next...

[2] Just a minute, Tony, my dear. Let me get rid of this annoying little man.

[3] This annoying little man will take that as Your Highness's leave to depart. I wish you good day, madam.

presence, and into the street, and, indeed, halfway back to the inn before I felt my pulse begin to moderate.

Perhaps I could have been – shall we say – more diplomatic, but I cannot see how the outcome would have differed in any significant way.

Your Lordship speaks Italian like a native (a native of several different cities as the need may be, if our sister Margaret is to be believed – as I am sure she is), and has travelled extensively throughout the Mediterranean, and will already have reached his own conclusions. For my part, the import of the scene I had witnessed could not be mistaken, especially as I had already recognised the distinctive pipe from my travels in the Levant, where the use of the poppy is as widespread as that of *Nicotiana tabacum*.

I must therefore inform your Lordship of the unwelcome news that your Lordship's contact in Florence is currently in exile (possibly self-imposed, possibly not, for reasons political unknown or for reasons personal that speak for themselves) from the city.

His wife, meanwhile, is an habitual opium eater and apparently prey to some species of gigolo.

Your Lordship will form his own conclusions as to the suitability of these persons to be entrusted in future with confidential information.

Your Lordship will also forgive me if I decline to place any reliance during my stay in Tuscany on the princely house of Cosadetti, but prefer to manage my visit on my own resources and those of my family.

Please be assured that it is with extreme reluctance that I pass on this news, and that this unfortunate event in no way effects the gratitude for your Lordship's endeavours that is, and will always be felt by,

Your Lordship's firm friend,

F. Bennet.

Chapter Seventeen : Mr Bennet to Mrs Darcy – Florentine Weather

Florence
21 October 1836

Dear Lizzie,

No matter what Botticelli may have painted, Venus certainly did not rise from the waves in Florence. Not without instant double pneumonia, at any rate.

Genoa was positively sultry, and I should have been content to spend more time there, but it did not suit the physical powers that be, nor the steamer schedule, and we must proceed direct to Leghorn and hence straight to the capital of the Grand Duchy.

Florence is picturesque enough, to be sure, especially the surrounding countryside, which looks suspiciously like the background to a painting by Filipino Lippi or Leonardo, but it is freezing cold. The tall narrow streets are designed to be impenetrable by the harmful rays of the sun, and I swear I have been warmer in the ice house at Pemberley. And the wind that blows constantly through the narrow gaps between the buildings could only be grateful to an Esqimau.

The *Albergo dello Scudo de Francia* has deserved Pennworth's recommendation in almost every respect. The rooms are spacious, comfortable and well furnished. The servants are attentive and apparently trustworthy, and the food is edible.

It suffers from the same shortcoming as the rest of the city, however. *Colonia Aemilia Florentia*, the ancient Roman town, benefited from the convenience of the hypocaust. The heating arrangements of its modern counterpart have only declined over the last two thousand years, however. Nowhere in all the plethora of cold, draughty palaces does one see so much as the kind of rudimentary fireplace that the meanest cottage in England could boast, and these massive piles rely for remaining habitable on chafing dishes, that is to say, bowls of charcoal smouldering away to shed the semblance of heat over all the surrounding six inches.

The masterpieces of art to be seen in these palaces, and in the churches, and even on the streets are, quite literally, breathtaking, but one is invariably obliged to abandon their study sooner than one would like by the intrusion of some cicerone-cum-bearleader leading his client by the nose through the obligatory round of compulsory classics, or by some passing native barging past without so much as a by-your-leave. I had forgotten that the Italians are simply incapable of leaving sufficient space for comfort between themselves and any other person, which makes it impossible for an Englishman to remain immobile unless his back is against a wall.

Margaret, of course, is in ecstasies wherever she goes, or, at least, when she is not in agonies of indecision as to which *capolavoro* to copy next. You will notice I am already beginning to drop the odd word in Italian into the mixture. I shall be a bona fide grand tourist yet.

In fact, I mean to climb Brunelleschi's dome tomorrow, as an earnest of how much improved my breathing is by James Morland's prescription.

Perhaps that will convince everyone, at last, that I am no longer an invalid.

Until then, I must remain

Your officially no more than convalescent father,

F. Bennet.

Chapter Eighteen : Mrs Bingley to Mrs Darcy – Worrying News

Florence
28 October 1836

Dear Lizzie,

I beg you to forgive me for not writing for so long. I could make all sorts of excuses, but the truth is that Papa has been very ill, and I was torn between whether to tell you immediately or spare you the worry we all shared until we knew whether we should fear the very worst or not.

I am satisfied now that I did the right thing in waiting, for he is much better now, up and about again and, as he puts it himself, being as much trouble as may be.

But I cannot begin to tell you how terribly worried I was, at first. I truly believe that if we had not had James Morland with us we should now be making our way back to you with Papa embalmed in a box. We very nearly had to do without the doctor, as it was, for he had been gone nearly a week, to consult a colleague in Bologna and only got back after Papa had already retired.

It all began so suddenly, too. Papa had been professing himself much improved, and had been showing it, too. He had been striding about the city with all his old vigour, and had even climbed the steps to the top of the dome in the cathedral that morning. He did so, moreover, without ever stopping for a rest, or complaining about being out of breath, although his colour at the top was rather higher than at the bottom. Pray do not suspect me of a pun, Lizzie. You know quite well what I mean.

For the rest of the day he never complained once about his chest, which made it something of an epoch in our journey, and I went to sleep with a lighter heart than I had done since we came to Florence.

I was woken the next morning by Arianna running into the room crying out that the master was dying.

Flinging on my *peignoir*, I followed her to Papa's room, where I found him tossing and turning in the bed, his eyes wide and staring, and his face the colour of old burgundy. And all the while he was racked with such a bout of coughing as I had never seen before. I say 'coughing' for want of a more succinct word, but it was as much wheezing and choking as coughing. His colour deepened even as I watched, and he was quite unable to speak in reply to my questions.

"Quick," I said to Arianna, "run and fetch the Doctor. Thank God he got back from Bologna last night."

The choking and wheezing increased with every second that passed, and I was truly beginning to fear the worst when James Morland arrived, with Margaret following.

He wasted no time on professional tutting and grunting, but called instantly upon Arianna to bring Mr Bingley with the utmost urgency.

"Si, signore," she replied. "Shall I inform Madama Bennet, too?"

"Best not, just yet," I replied. "Let us not alarm her needlessly."

"I will not speculate about the immediate cause of this seizure," said James, while we were waiting, "but it is clear that something is obstructing Mr Bennet's airway and he cannot breath. If we allow this to continue, there can be only one end. I believe that he has been ignoring his pulmonary congestion in my absence, and it has spread so that it is now blocking his windpipe while he lies on his back. We must turn him over so that he lies prone, when his windpipe will be, I hope, above the level of the fluid in his lungs and he will be able to breathe again. Once he is easy in his breathing I will have time to investigate further, but this must be done at once or there will be no hope."

"What must be done at once?" enquired Charles, squeezing into the room, which was becoming rather crowded.

"We must turn Papa over onto his front," I told him. "Don't ask why; there is no time. Just do it."

Charles is a happily married man, and knows what that involves. He said nothing, but immediately took Papa's right arm, while James took his left.

"Feel free to assist, ladies," grunted the Doctor, "for no-one could ever accuse Mr Benett of being a lightweight, in any sense of the word."

We heaved and we tugged and we hoisted, and eventually got Papa onto his front.

The difference was remarkable. The choking ceased almost instantly, although the coughing abated but little. But, slowly, the purple colour faded from that dear face.

"Good!" pronounced James. "I should not like to have had to perform a trachaeotomy so far from home. Now, let us see."

And he proceeded to do all the things we should expect, with his watch and his hand on Papa's wrist, and his Fahrenheit's tube, and his little ear trumpet.

"It is as I thought," he said. "There is a hectic fever in addition to the old symptoms, possibly from the miasma arising from the river. We should consider removing to higher ground, but we must await the crisis first. I could wish my medicine chest were better stocked, but I did not foresee so many calls upon it."

"Oh, James!" Margaret chided. "We are in the city of the Medici. Surely there are medicines to be had here?"

"I dare say you are right, my love, but...Italian apothecaries! I have no notion of them."

"And what of Doctor Balanzone? You went to consult an Italian physician not a million years ago."

"A physician is not an apothecary. Still...you are right, my love, of course. Arianna, *corre allo speziale lo piu cercano e...* Forgive me, I forget, your Italian is the best of us all, of course. Run to the nearest apothecary and ask if he has any Dover's Powder -*Pulvis Doveri* -. If he has, fetch me four ounces. If he has not, ask for Syrup of Ipecac, or Brazil Root. Here is half a guinea."

With no more than the traditional *'subito, Dottore,'* she was gone, and we must now wait.

And wait was what most of us did for the next week, most of us females, that is, for the gentlemen had better things to do, although Doctor Morland, to do him justice, did look in regularly, and check that his prescription was being consumed, and make one vital intervention. The day to day and night to night attendance to the little necessities and indignities were, naturally, women's work, however.

Pray forgive the peevish tone. Two solid weeks of shift work, six till two, followed by two till ten, followed by ten till six will have that effect, I find. How we should have managed without Arianna I do not know. She enabled us to do eight hour shifts instead of twelve. She it was who found the syrup of Ipecac for the Doctor, having searched every apothecary in the city, it seemed.

I cannot believe that Wyckham was all set to turn her off, having enticed her all the way from Corfu to take charge of his children, simply because she was surplus to requirements now that they were all at school. Papa did a good thing when he engaged her to look after Mama.

Mama did try to help at first, but we persuaded her to take care of her own health instead, 'as what should we do if you were laid low like poor Mr Bennet?' She was not unwilling to be persuaded, and, fortunately, found a new friend in Mr Landor, an English poet, whom she met at Mr Arbuthnot's one day, and who turned out to be a great admirer of Margaret's work, so great, indeed, that he allowed her to induce him to occupy Mama in assisting her to select new lodgings. She could be much more usefully occupied there than in the sickroom, as you may imagine.

I have let this letter go on too long, have I not? My excuse is that I must unburden myself somehow. Charles will not hear anything about even the mildest illness, and, while Margaret and Arianna are willing ears, they cannot feel about Papa as you and I do, my Lizzie.

Forgive me for taking advantage, my dear. I should scrap this letter and start again, but that we shall not have such a chance of a swift delivery again, and you must be told the news.

And the news now is all good, I assure you. There was one frightening incident, the second day after James's return, when Papa, under the influence of constant applications of ipecac, coughed up such a great gobbet of bloody mucus as was bigger than my fist, far bigger than I should have thought possible, but that turned out to be just what the doctor ordered.

"The constant application of small doses of ipecac has had the expectorant effect I wished for," said James when he was summoned to the scene. "It has cleared the blockage in Mr Bennet's lungs. He will do well now."

And he has done well. He has done so well that we are now about to remove to new lodgings. The removal is for the sake of Papa's health, to be sure, but the very fact that we can contemplate it is proof that he is on the mend.

So I tell myself, at any rate, and so I tell you, my beloved sister. But I do not say so merely for general reassurance and consolation, but because I genuinely believe it to be true. James Morland believes it, too, so you may take it that I have good authority for my conviction.

Write back with all of your news as soon as you may. We are all at that stage in a foreign trip where the constant, unremitting foreignness of everything is starting to get us down. Margaret tells me the feeling will pass, and I am sure she is right. She has had far more experience of this sort of thing than I have. But, as it is, I long to hear more of your doings at Pemberly. News of Garthdale and even Meryton would not come amiss, too.

We have still found no sign of Frank and Mina. I believe Papa is writing to Lord Pennworth, and he may have news that has not reached us yet. You may be sure I shall pass on anything I hear.

I shall write you a more cheerful letter next time, Lizzie, I promise, and in that sure and certain hope you may trust,

Your loving sister,

Jane.

Chapter Nineteen: Mrs Darcy to Mrs Bingley – Entreaties

Pemberley
5 November 1836

Dear, reliable Jane,

Of course I do not doubt your word, never for one moment, but I long to be told, over and over again, even, that our father is restored to his old, accustomed health at last, and I beg you, I implore you to indulge me in that fancy.

The reading of your last letter provoked more alarms and shivers of the spine than Miss Shelley's novel. It very nearly provoked the excursions to match the alarms, too, for Fitzwilliam was all for the Chiltern Hundreds and the next ship to Livorno, laden with every pill, potion and nostrum known to mankind, not forgetting Bingley's Bronchial Balsam.

I pointed out the great disappointment that such a course would occasion in the county, and the danger of his dereliction letting in some radical incomer, perhaps a mere democrat, perhaps even an advocate of universal suffrage or some other unnatural cause.

Moreover, it had evidently escaped my beloved's notice that their Aunt Jane was at present rather inconveniently placed to take charge of the children in our absence. Indeed, we were currently entrusted with her own, and neither Kitty, nor Lydia, nor even Mary could be thought to be an acceptable substitute.

These arguments proved irresistible. I know not whether it was universal suffrage or Lydia that did the trick, but he at last consented to do his duty, although he still talks of sending a consignment to you of, at least, the famous Balsam.

But, in all seriousness, Jane, we know each other, you and I, and we know Papa. We know the hole his absence would make in our world. I trust you entirely, completely, and implicitly. You say that Papa is on the way to recovery; I rejoice. I ask only that you inform me, instantly, of any turn for the worse. My feelings would much rather be alarmed than spared, and the Leghorn boat may yet find itself with an extra passenger or two.

In the sure and certain hope that that particular cabin will remain unoccupied, you may always rely upon,

Your impatient little sister,

Elizabeth.

Chapter Twenty : Mrs Bingley to Mrs Darcy - Reassurance

Dear Lizzie,

My last letter was a terrible piece of self-indulgence, and actually sending it was even worse. I wish I could be sure that it left you truly rejoicing. I believe you, of course, just as much as you believe me, but I somehow feel that we both would be happier with more evidence on which to base our belief.

Perhaps this will do? During the worst days of his seizure, Papa was at first entirely unable to speak, and then for a while completely incoherent, under the influence of the laudanum with which the Doctor was dosing him for the fever. We kept constant watch, of course, for the crisis. I remember precisely the moment the fever broke, and we knew the battle was won, for I witnessed it myself, and marked the time on my watch. I had been dozing off in the chair by Papa's bedside when I suddenly noticed he was no longer tossing and turning, and immediately feared the worst.

I started up, and instantly felt for his pulse, as James had shown us all how to do. It was calm, and firm, and his skin was no longer red hot to the touch. His breathing was much more regular, too, almost normal. Looking up, I saw that his eyes were open, and fixed upon me.

"Jane, my dear," he said, "what do you here?"

"Oh, Papa," I sobbed, "you have been very ill. We thought you were going to die."

"Die, my dear?" he replied, "Why, that is the last thing I shall do."

With those words I knew that we had our own dear Papa back with us, and need fear no more for him.

And so it has been established, for his recovery has proved remarkably rapid. James is now perfectly satisfied of his patient's ability to withstand the rigours of our onward journey. Which is just as well, since Papa is now perfectly out of humour with Florence, on whose chill winds and shady streets he blames his relapse. Whether the climate of Rome will suit him better remains to be seen, but it is to Rome that we must go, and Charles has arranged passage on the next steamboat from Leghorn to Civitavecchia. He may be useless in the sick room, but he knows his shipping agents.

So I bid you be of good cheer, my love, and it will probably be from the Eternal City that you next hear from

Your relieved and thankful sister,

Jane B.

Chapter Twenty-one : Mr Bennet to Mrs Darcy – Paternal Vows

Florence

5 November 1836

My own, dear Lizzie,

Jane showed me your letter, by which I was strangely touched.

Forgive me for not writing sooner, but I confess I have not been very well lately. Pray do not concern yourself, however. Jane made much of it, and Morland fussed about, but I am perfectly recovered now. Still, Florence and I do not suit each other, I fear.

With the assistance of Mr Landor, however, we are now removed to an apartment in the Oltrarno, south of the river, and much airier while at the same time more sheltered, and I begin to recover myself.

In fact, I do believe I have at last found a convenient spot to take the air. There is a corner of the Boboli Gardens which catches the sun of an afternoon, sheltered by the circumambient hedges from the icy blasts of the eternal north wind where a wandering English invalid may sit, swathed in rugs, and contemplate the view, while listening to the chatter of the goldfinches almost drowning the wheezing of his lungs.

James Morland seems pleased that I can get up here on my own two legs, and, to tell the truth, I am rather pleased myself, too. I should not like to have to look for a bath chair in Florence, so it is just as well that I am not quite ready for one yet.

It is amazing the difference that can be made by an hour or two sitting in the sun in a sheltered nook. It is almost as if the rays of the sun were truly as life-giving as the ancients believed them to be.

Sitting here, I could very nearly get to like Florence, but it does not signify, since we are to move on to Rome the day after tomorrow. James Morland believes the weather here does not answer his purpose, so we must move further south.

I cannot argue with him on that point, and am the less inclined to do so since I have concluded that to stay longer would make no difference to my researches. The Laurentian Library has proved strangely disappointing and I must hope for more from the Vatican.

We attend upon Mr Arbuthnot for his soirée tomorrow night and the following morning to Leghorn to take ship to Civitavecchia. You may see how fully recovered I am by my contemplation of these antics with such a degree of equanimity.

Your mother will enjoy herself, I make no doubt, and perhaps Jane and Margaret will too. I dare say Charles and James between them will keep them happily occupied on the dance floor, while your mother allows her new friend Mr Landor to flatter her while quietly taking notes for his next satirical verse.

For my own part, I shall sit unobtrusively in a corner and watch my neighbours making sport for me, for a change, and think of my dear Lizzie, who shows far too much concern for

Her undeserving father,

F. Bennet.

Chapter Twenty-two : Mrs Bennet to Mrs Darcy – Literature

Leghorn
6 November 1836

Dear Lizzie,

I write you this line before we go on board yet another steamship that will take us all to Civitavecchia for Rome. Why it does not take us direct to Rome itself I cannot say. 'Is not Rome on the famous River Tiber?' I ask. 'If steamships come upriver to London, why may they not go upriver to Rome?'

'Ah, but the Tiber is not the Thames', is all the answer I get. Of course the Tiber is not the Thames. If it were, then Rome would be London, and we should not have had to come all this way. That is perfectly plain, but when I ask for further explanation they wax all technical, talking of tides, and sandbanks, and currents and such stuff, and my mind refuses to follow.

Now I think of it, it can only be because it does not suit the captains and shipowners to spend more on coal than is absolutely necessary, which is a pity, but perfectly understandable, unlike tides and currents and sand banks.

I do not know that I much care for these steamboats myself. They are convenient, to be sure, and much more regular and reliable than the old sailing ships, but they are so smelly and dirty. If ever you want thoroughly to ruin a good muslin dress, wear it on a voyage on a steamship. You may be sure you will never get the smuts out.

The gentlemen, of course, never think of such practical matters. Their talk, while on board, is all of cylinders and pistons and pressures and such, which always strikes me as perfectly incomprehensible as well as somewhat indelicate.

But why have you so induced me to rattle on about steam ships in this way, Lizzie? I am sure neither of us have any interest in such things, and now I must think to remember what I meant to say. You always were a most provoking child!

Oh, yes! It was to tell you to look out for a new book that is to come out in London soon, and order me a copy. It is called *Pericles and Aspasia,* and is by my great friend Mr Landor, who is a very well-known poet, so everyone tells me, but not much appreciated by the booksellers. We met Mr Landor in Florence, and he was very kind to me there, showing me quite as much attention as your father failed to show me, he being encouraged by Jane and the Morlands to think himself at death's door and so given the perfect excuse to avoid all the parties and balls.

I dare say you think your poor old mother far too old to care for balls and parties, Lizzie? Well, I will let you into a secret. It is only when one's daughters are safely married, when they are 'off your hands', as Lady Lucas would say, such a vulgar expression I always used to think, but then the Lucases were never anything but trade until poor Charlotte's father got himself knighted, and now Charlotte herself is just waiting for the day she can turn me out of Longbourn as Mrs Collins. Still, she will never be anything but *Mrs* Collins and my daughter is *Lady* Wyckham, which is a comfort, to be sure, but there you go again, Lizzie, you have turned me from my subject. You always were a provoking child.

Now, what was I saying? Oh, yes, it is only when you have safely married all your daughters, when you have done your duty, that you can really begin to enjoy balls and parties. You will say that when you are *jeune fille en fleur* (yes, I can quote French too, you know) your pleasure in such things can never again be equalled, but, even then, you are competing, you must impress, you must attach, you are thinking of other people's pleasure as well as your own. But when you get to a certain age, when you have nothing left either to prove or gain, *that* is when you can begin to enjoy these things for their own sake, and for your own sake, too.

I cannot begin to tell you how much pleasure it gives your old mother to be sought after again, even if it is only for a turn around the dance floor, and praised for her elegance and charm, however insincerely. Your father is a very wise and learned man – in great things - but a small matter such as this has never been within his understanding. He tells me it is all vanity and flattery, without perceiving that it is things such as these that help the world go round. I shall miss Mr Landor when we are in Rome.

Pray let me know what you think of Mr Landor's book. I have a secret notion that he may have based the character of Aspasia upon me. Writers do that sort of thing, you know. I know nothing of the real Aspasia myself, or Pericles, other than that they were both very famous antique Romans (or was it Greeks? I can never tell the difference). Your father was very willing to enlighten me on the subject when I asked him, and proceeded to do so at terribly excessive length, but I fear none of it sank in.

I think your father is perhaps a little jealous of Mr Landor. I know they did not get on so very well when last they met. They fell to talking about poetry, about modern poetry, and you know what your father thinks of that. Mr Landor was praising the modern romantic, while your father was maintaining that there had not been a poet worthy the name in the English language since Milton.

"But, surely," Mr Landor was saying, "when one considers the works of Byron, Shelley, Coleridge..."

"Shelley!" your father sniffed, "his work borders on the incoherent, and Coleridge's strays well over that border all too often. As for Lord Byron, I have friends in the Morea who think very highly of him, but not at all for his poetical works."

"What of Wordsworth, then? Is he not a poet of surpassing stature?"

"Of Mr Wordsworth's verses I can think of no better appraisal than Cicero's on those of Lucretius. *'Multis luminibus ingenii, non tamen artis.'*[4] He has his moments, but so much of his stuff is mere fustian. I could do as well myself, extempore, for most of it."

"I challenge you then, Mr Bennet. Taking one of Wordsworth's as your model, to extemporise upon it, on the spot, here and now."

We all expected your father to yield at this point, but he never ceases to amaze me.

---

[4] With many flashes of genius but not so much skill.

"Very well," he replied, "let me see. I will leave it to you to divine my model."

And instantly he began reciting–

"I wandered silent as a mouse
That creeps about from house to house,
When, on a bankside I saw lots,
A host of blue forget-me-nots,
Or myosotis in the Greek –
That's 'mouseface', if you English speak.
That name Miss Otis straight recalled
A maid who once held me enthralled.
She spurned me, and left me forlorn,
And wishing I had ne'er been born.
The reason why, I know not what,
Yet hope that she'll forget me not."

I felt so proud of your father just then. That he should produce such a finished verse, on the spot, just like that, every bit as good as the famous Mr Wordsworth's! How lucky I have been to have him as my husband, how lucky you all have been to have him as your father!

Mr Landor found fault, of course.

"Mere doggerel!" he asserted.

"I do not doubt it," replied Mr Bennet, "But is it any more so than the original?"

The argument now quite lost me, with all its talk of rhyme schemes, and meters and *enjambements* and such. I feared we should see no more of Mr Landor after that, for you know how savage your father is with his set downs, but we remained friends for all that, which is just as well, for I should not have liked to have been obliged to break off my outings with Mr Landor.

After all, it is not as if your father ever did anything but sit in libraries and poke about in old churches while we were in Florence. Whenever there was anything going on in the evening he would be overcome by his cough, and insist on absorbing the Morlands – or, at least, Mrs Morland for the evening, to attend him.

Thank goodness I had your sister Jane to keep me company among the wallflowers, and Mr Landor to lead me round the floor from time to time, for a lady cannot always be dancing with her relatives, you know.

Do not bother to send Mr Landor's book on, however, for the expense, I fear, would be prodigious, and, in any case, we shall be home, I dare say, in the spring, when the sight of your face, and the faces of my lovely grandchildren will bring joy to the heart of

Your loving mother,

Jane Bennet.

Chapter Twenty-three : Mrs Morland to Mrs Darcy - Medical Experiments

Rome
10 November 1836

My Dear Elizabeth,

I find myself challenged as to how to begin this letter- indeed, how to continue from the beginning for that matter- but I think it had best be written, so I can think of nothing better than to plunge straight in.

I write to you for advice on what to do to ease a – I will not call it an estrangement- but a cooling in relations between myself and your father.

It all sprang from a foolish – and quite accidental - concatenation of circumstances, which I fear I may have made worse by my attitude at the time. I value greatly my friendship with Mr Bennet, and almost think of him as my own father, whom I barely remember, and wish to do everything I can to heal this breach.

But, what am I to do? He avoids me at all times. He barely speaks to me, save for the merest polite formalities, and there is no one else here I may speak to without causing more embarrassment all round.

I had better explain the circumstances, had I not?

Your father has lately been undergoing a course of treatment prescribed by my husband, after his consultations in Bologna with Doctor Balanzone, a course of treatment of a somewhat experimental nature, which involves exposure of the skin to the beneficial rays of the sun. To obtain the greatest benefit, as much of the skin as possible must be exposed, and Mr Bennet has become accustomed to lying on a daybed on the roof terrace here for half an hour every day, with only a sheet to preserve his modesty.

To give James due credit, the process seems to have benefited Mr Bennet considerably, for he hardly coughs at all now.

Last week, the morning before we were to go to the Orsinis in the evening, Arianna had washed my best white petticoat and left it out in the sun to dry and bleach. Having sent her out for some ribbon, and wishing to try on my dress for the evening, I absent-mindedly went on the roof for my petticoat, forgetting that Mr Bennet was out there, and disturbed him in a state of nature, his sheet having blown away in the breeze while he dozed.

I attempted to escape without arousing him, but I must have made some noise, for he awoke and saw me there, and fell into a great state of confusion, searching for his missing sheet and apologising over and over for any offence his state might have given.

I attempted to make light of it, saying, as near as I can remember the words.

"It is I who must apologise to you, sir, for disturbing you thus. It was unintentional, I assure you, for I wished only to get my petticoat."

He insisted on there being some offence to atone for, however, and I must continue –

"I beg you, Mr Bennet let there be no more of such talk. I assure you I am not at all offended.

Do not mind me, I pray. I am a country doctor's wife, who has assisted her husband in attending patients. Moreover, I am a painter, who has attended life classes at the Academy. Ladies may do that, you know, as long as they do not expect to receive any credit for their attendance. I assure you I have seen nothing here that I have not seen many times before."

It was in some attempt at soothing his wounded feelings, I assure you, that made me add -

"I must congratulate you, however, on having retained the physique you have. I have seen many a model twenty years younger who looked in far worse state."

Had I left things there, we might have got back onto a normal footing sooner. But something prompted me to continue-

"In fact, er... you would not care to wait just a little while, so that I may get my sketch pad? It is just that look on your face, all shock and horror and embarrassment, combined with just the merest hint of concupiscence, it cries out to me to capture it. I suppose you would not consent to sit for me? I should put a beard on your chin, and lots of hair on your head and call it 'Pericles surprised by Aspasia' or some such thing, and get myself hung among the History Paintings at last. No one would recognise you, you may count on that."

At this point I realised that I had said too much, and, pausing only to make a rough sketch with the materials I had at the time (that petticoat has never been the same since), I mumbled some few words of apology and fled.

Since then, things have been between us as I said. I could excuse my verbosity by saying my artistic soul was overwhelmed, but the truth is that I was well-nigh as embarrassed as Mr Bennet, and when I am embarrassed I tend to babble. James is quite the opposite. When he finds himself in an embarrassing situation he becomes not so much tongue-tied as completely dumb. I, on the other hand, go on and on, much as I am doing now, and never know when to stop.

So, there you are, Lizzie. You have both my confession and my plea for absolution, and it is to you that I leave my penance. How can I make amends? What shall I do?

You are Mr Bennet's favourite daughter, and, I think, the most sensible. Sensible enough, I hope, not to let this confession lower me too much in your estimation, and to give me the benefit of the doubt and your counsel. If *you* cannot think of a way to restore our relations to a normal footing, who can?

I am sorry to be so demanding, but it is a token of how highly I value both your father's friendship and yours.

Write to me soon, and ease the heart of

Your repentant friend,

Margaret Morland

Chapter Twenty-four :   Mrs Darcy to Mrs Morland – On Confidence

Pemberley

20 November 1836

My dear Margaret,

What a delight it was to read your letter. It was almost like something from one of your novels. I dare say it will be, one of these days.

I am glad to hear that James's new treatment has done Papa some good. We have all been worrying, especially since neither the sea voyage nor your stay in Florence seem to have helped. Let us hope that the Roman climate will prove more congenial, or at least that being surrounded by so many memorials of his beloved antiquity will rouse him to recover his health.

I must confess that the very thought of being able to lie out in the sun makes me wish I had come with you after all. The view of the hills surrounding Pemberley, all white with snow at this time of year, and the sky all covered with grey clouds, does not encourage such activities, I fear. We must go to London soon for the next session, but I dare say the weather there will be very little better.

I laughed out loud when I read your account of your *little contretemps.* Now I must think how to reply to your questions. What can I say?

First of all, I will say, quite clearly, that your confiding in me has not lowered you in my estimation. Quite the contrary; it must have taken no little amount of courage to make your confession, and I honour you for it. In future, let there be no more such scruples. I fully intend to say anything I wish to you, and I expect you to do the same to me. Let that be the penance you requested.

As for absolution, I doubt very much that you need it. If I know my own father, he will secretly be rather gratified that you paid him the compliment of asking him to model for one of your paintings. He would never dream of mentioning it again himself, but I do not think he would take it amiss if it were brought to his attention again.

I will not pretend to advise, still less to instruct you what to do next. Your own sense will guide you unerringly, I am sure. I will tell you what I would do, however. I would make a point of asking him whether he had given your suggestion any more thought. I leave it to you whether to elaborate on how useful and convenient it would be for you, how there could be no more appropriate setting for your labours, how it could be the making of your reputation etc. You might also devote some thought as to whether the subject might best be broached in private or in front of witnesses, say, at mealtimes or some other convenient instance. I have said I will not tell you what to do, and I will not, but you will forgive me if I say you ought to do something. To use an analogy from your husband's profession, better to lance the boil now than wait until it bursts.

I may be quite wrong, of course, and it may slowly subside of its own accord. Do they not say 'least said, soonest mended?' But I do not think I am wrong in being confident that, however you deal with this embarrassment, you will deal with it skilfully and with the least possible fuss.

Have you really heard nothing from, or of Frank and Mina? They should have been in Rome a good while now, and the circles in which English tourists move cannot surely be quite so large as completely to miss each other. Perhaps they have moved on to Naples?

If you do hear anything, please pass it on as soon as you can, to soothe the maternal fears of

Your highly entertained friend- and sister of sorts, remember,

Elizabeth Darcy

Chapter Twenty-five: Mr Bennet to Mrs Darcy - A New Career

Albergo del Tonno

14 December 1836

Dear Lizzie,

You will be pleased to hear that today we celebrated an epoch. It is a full month since I last wheezed or coughed, and Morland has pronounced my lungs free from congestion.

In fact, I feel positively well, so well that I have embarked upon a new career. What, you say, so late in life, to start out anew? You will never guess what my new calling is.

I am become an artist's model. I do not sit in an art school while students draw me, nor do I travel from one studio to another, nor am I even paid for my trouble, but that is what I am, nonetheless. Margaret Morland is the painter, of course. She has persuaded me to sit for an historical painting for her. I thought the myth of such things being the ultimate in the painter's career had been exploded long ago, but apparently not.

The new work is to be called '*Pericles and Aspasia*,' and I am the Athenian statesman, of course. Who Margaret will find to model for the famous *hetaera* I have no idea. I cannot think that your sister Jane will allow herself to be persuaded, even though we may all be discovering previously hidden corners of our own temperaments.

I must admit I had my doubts at first, but now that I have tried it I find it very congenial employment. Had I known sooner that I could be paid for sitting in the sun on a roof terrace in Italy, swathed in a sheet, while a handsome young lady chats with me and dabs paint on a canvas I should have taken up the profession long since.

Margaret does not pay me, of course, but, then, I have never paid her for the many hours she has devoted to nursing me, nor the even more hours of amusement she has provided over the years. With you and Jane both gone, I believe I should have gone mad in Meryton without someone to engage in sensible conversation.

Rome is proving very nearly as disappointing as Florence, as far as my research goes. We travel the world in search of I know not what, when we should do just as well if we sat quietly at home. I fear I must be getting old.

However, I have heard tell of secret grottoes and caverns beneath the hill next to the Colosseum which have lain unexplored since the time of the Caesars. Your mother's new young man is a Roman born, and tells me he knows someone who could guide me to subterranean wonders previously unknown to the learned world.

I confess that I am very tempted to take him up on his offer. The only thing that gives me pause is a foolish reluctance to owe anything to Count Posca, and thus give your mother more excuse for indulging him.

If Frank and Mina ever were in Rome, no-one in the English community, nor among the physical nor artistic sets ever laid eyes upon them. I suppose I could use Mina's uncle's letter of introduction to try and find out more. It is addressed to some cardinal, however, and I am reluctant to associate so closely with Papistry. I am also loath to waste my time after that fiasco in Florence.

We may have a new direction when I write to you next, for we are even now a-hunting for lodgings, or an apartment in a more fashionable area. We have only viewed one possibility so far, close by the Spanish Steps, said to have been inhabited in the past by *'un scrittore Famoso Inglese'*, but it felt rather damp to me, quite unsuitable for someone with a chest complaint, and in any case it was far too small.

However, I hope to have some news soon.

Until then, do not forget

Your loving and almost gainfully employed

Father,

F. Bennet.

Chapter Twenty-six : Mrs Bingley to Mrs Darcy – Bringing Up Parents.

Viale del Pincio
21 December 1836

Dear Lizzie,

There has been such a change in Papa since we came to Rome that you would barely recognise him.

All his life, I believe, certainly all our lives, he has been an observer, rather than a participator. Others do; he sits back and watches, and comments on their actions.

For him to act himself has been vanishingly rare. I can think only of when he went to London in search of Lydia and Wyckham before they were married. But, now, he has thrown himself into this Roman Art project of his. We never see him from one day's end to the next, and all he talks about are his discoveries. And now he has infected Margaret, too, taking her with him every day, so that she spends much less time on her own work, which I have something of an interest in. But I must not say more on that point as yet.

I am sure that in his own role of observer he would not be happy with the way Count Posca is ... attending on – I almost said 'courting' our mother.

I know that I am not happy with it, and I have told him so, but you know Papa. "Your mother will never be easy in this city till she has exposed herself in some public place or another, and we can never expect her to do it with so little expense or inconvenience to her family as under the present circumstances." I cannot help remembering another occasion on which he used almost identical words, and can only hope that similar consequences will not ensue.

We are removed, as you can see, to a new apartment on the Pincian Hill, much more airy and less smelly than where we previously were, with a view down towards Castel Sant'Angelo. Doctor Morland pronounces it a much healthier neighbour hood than where we were, down by the river and subject to the ague-inducing miasmas.

Papa laments the proximity to the remains, which cannot be denied; we had but to walk out of the front door to find ourselves across the square from the Pantheon. Even he, however, allows that 'the Campus Martius was a notoriously unhealthy area', although he does tend to quote, if I remember correctly, Cicero and Suetonius as authority rather than anything more recent.

The rest of us find we are perfectly suited. Bingley likes the proximity of more English families. The Morlands rejoice in the extra space. Margaret has her own studio now, while the Doctor has a room of his own where he may conduct his experiments. As for mama, she is still debating whether Rome is in Italy or Italy in Rome, and all she asks is to be convenient for the palazzi of the black nobility, as the ancient Roman families are called, where she devotes her evenings, after a day spent shopping with Arianna, to obtaining an entrée by means of her young count.

The young count is another subject, and if I start on him I will still be writing when Christmas comes. We are all concerned about him, and think him no addition. Like his aunt, the Marchesa, he always happens to turn up at mealtimes, and never seems to be quite properly turned out for the soirées to which Mama so loves to be conducted, so that she must needs buy him a pair of gloves, or a cravat pin, or some such trifle before they may attend.

And in the evenings – but, there I have started about the Count- Signor Contino, as Papa calls him, and must keep my promise to defer the subject for another occasion. But I cannot help wishing we had a second Figaro to teach him to dance elsewhere.

No matter. Enjoy your festivities at Pemberley. If you can find time, perhaps you might pop over to Garthdale to see how the Hursts are faring, but only if you have leisure and the weather permits.

Here, we know not whether to be amused or bemused at the local Christmas customs. We shall be attending the English Church, of course, but this being Italy, we often hear carols being sung in the streets, all of them very strange to our ears. There is only one that I have so far been able to catch, and even there I am restricted to the first line, '*Tu vieni del Cielo*' and the chorus '*Santa Natale, Bambino mio, Santa Natale, Santo Bambino*. It is a catchy, cheerful tune, and compares well to our dreary dirges.

While you are singing those at Pemberley, be sure that you are always in the thoughts of

Your loving sister

Jane.

Chapter Twenty-seven : Mrs Darcy to Mr Bennet – A Young Man?

Pemberley
22 December 1836

Dear Papa,

I am truly gratified to hear that you have found so congenial a pastime, and even more glad that your health seems to be improving.

But what is this about mother's 'new young man'? To hear of a new old man would have been quite startling enough, but a new young man? Whatever can you mean? Please tell me it is not what it sounds like. I have heard of the Italian custom of adopting what is called a *cicisbeo*, but I cannot in any way imagine Mama engaging in such a thing.

Mama as a femme fatale, or even as a lady of a certain age encouraging the attentions of a young man is an image I simply cannot form in my mind. In fact, I refuse even to think of it. Yet I *must* think of it.

Oh, papa, tell me I am wrong and that all is well between you and mama. Tell me soon, and ease the heart of

Your perplexed daughter,

Elizabeth.

Chapter Twenty-eight: Mrs Bingley to Lady Wyckham -Roman Scandals

Rome

2 January 1837

Dear Lydia,

We have finally made our entrée into Roman Society. This was not as easy as we had expected, for, unlike Tuscany, there is no British Embassy to the Holy See, and therefore no obvious place for travellers from our nation to meet and hear about each other. Unless you already know someone, it is very difficult to make new acquaintances. There are no assembly rooms where one can be introduced by the Master of Ceremonies, and the only way to meet people is to accost perfect strangers in cafes. It seems a very odd way to go on, but that is what happens.

I am sure that we would have found things easier if your father would only use the letter of introduction he has from Lord Pennworth, but he will not give himself the trouble. He was disappointed in his reception in Florence and refuses to repeat the experience. Still, perhaps it was just as well, for the letter is addressed to a Popish priest, and one hears so many tales about them. I remember my mama reading to me out of Fox's Martyrs. I should not like to find myself converted by mistake or even worse. The Papists are such wicked creatures. They are everywhere in Rome, however, even their Pope lives just across the river, with the most grandiose cathedral you

have ever seen, which your father tells me is merely
the Pope's private chapel. Such wealth and
ostentation one sees all around, my darling, and yet
there are beggars everywhere and the streets are
piled with filth. It would not do in England.

It was through being accosted ourselves
while sitting outside a café near yet another
Roman ruin that we first began to get to know
people in this city. We spent a lot of time sitting
outside cafes when we first came to Rome. It is
the done thing, apparently. I would have thought
it would be more comfortable to sit inside, but
that is what they say. They also say that one meets
people at cafes, but we must have tried every one
within walking distance of the inn, and never once
did anyone other than beggars importune us.

It is such a shame it is impossible to get a
decent cup of tea in these places. They do a very
strange kind of coffee, however, with whipped
cream floating on the top, which they call
Cappuccino. Marchesa Cacciasoldi tells me it was
only recently brought into Rome by the Austrians,
who call it Kapuziner. I remember the Austrians
very well from Venice. Rome is not quite so bad as
Venice, with obvious Austrian spies everywhere,
but I am sure the same little man has been
following me around for at least a week now, ever
since I met Count Posca.

Ah! Count Posca and Marchesa Cacciasoldi!
I have not told you about them, have I, Lydia,
dear? We met the Marchesa at a soirèe given by a
professional acquaintance of James Morland, one
Doctor Bartolo. These professional acquaintances
of the Doctor's were what we were forced to rely
upon for society, at first. The Doctor seems to
have acquaintances everywhere. Your father tells

me he is a great man in his own way, much caressed by the physical fraternity, but I cannot see it. He never dresses in any way out of the ordinary, nor gives himself airs, nor says anything particularly witty. Of course, when I was young, the physician came to the tradesmen's entrance, and was shown in via the kitchen. Now they are treated as if they were gentlemen, or at least members of the Royal Society. Some of them *are* gentlemen, of course. One certainly cannot fault James Morland on that head, as his sister-in-law is married to an earl, and his sister to a country gentleman of large and ancient estate in the west country. His mother is cousin to a duke, too, not that I care for such things, as you know.

But I am astray again. At Doctor Bartolo's evening I wore my blue tulle, with the peacock feather turban, and was greatly complemented by the gentlemen, but only one lady exerted herself enough even to acknowledge my existence with more than a curtsey.

"You are English, signora? I love the English, they are so calm, so polite, so generous! Ah! You must be the famosa Signora Bennet! I have so much heard of the new English family in Rome, the distinguished medico, the famous authoress, the eminent scholar and his so-elegant wife. But I say too much. We must not talk, no, for we have not yet been introduced? *Un attimo, per cortesia.*"

She crossed the room to Doctor Bartolo, whispered in his ear, and positively dragged him over from the corner where he was engaged in conversation with Doctor Morland.

"Signora Bennet," he addressed me, "I am amiss. I did not introduce you to my guest because

I made sure you were already known to her. Permit me to redress my fault. Marchesa Cacciasoldi, may I present to you Mrs Bennet, the wife of my English colleague's friend, Mr Bennet? I think you may have much to talk about."

Well, when we left the inn that evening, I had never expected to meet a marchioness, still less to find myself having a nice, comfortable coze with one. She spoke English very well, really, in a comical, foreign sort of way, and very soon we were chatting away as if we were old friends.

As you know, my love, I have never been one for idle chatter, nor for sharing confidences with complete strangers, but a marchioness is not just anyone, is she?

I thought nothing of it. One meets people at parties and then never sees them again, but she called on us the very next morning. She must have very early habits, for we were still at breakfast, and must invite her to join us, which she did with a will, doing full justice to the efforts of the innkeeper.

Since then, the Marchesa and I have become fast friends. She calls every day, usually at breakfast time, and we spend all day together, going to all the best shops and all the attractions with the best guides. She knows all the best eating-houses, too, and we never miss having lunch in one of them.

She never lets her rank go to her head, and spends all her time in charitable pursuits. The tales she tells of impoverished Roman gentlefolk, and the things they suffered at the hands of the wicked French! She is a true saint of these latter days, for she spends all her income assisting those less fortunate than herself. Her name must be blessed every day among the widows and orphans of the Eternal City. I help her from time to time with small gifts of money. She never asks for herself, but her charity is boundless, and I am always glad to be of assistance when I hear her stories. Besides, I never can remember what these foreign coins are worth, or even believe that they really are money, and anything I need at the shops I charge to your father's account, as I have always done.

I am surprised that Wyckham does not have accounts with many tradesmen. He does seem so terribly unlucky in that way. He always has so much trouble with wherever he shops, and even more with wherever you shop.

You must let me know what you should like me to bring you back from Rome. Now that Mr Bennet is so much better I dare say we shall be coming home soon, but I cannot say precisely when that will be.

Until then, remember that you are always in the thoughts of

Your loving mother,

J. Bennet.

P.S.

Happy New Year!

Chapter Twenty-nine: Lady Wyckham to Mrs Bennet - It must be terribly boring

Pemberley
10 January 1837

Dear Mama,

Thank you for your letter from Rome. It was fortunate it caught us still at Longbourn, for we are about to leave for Garthdale since there is no longer anything to keep us here.

I wish you, or, rather, Papa had left clearer instructions for Hill. He makes such a to-do whenever Wyckham calls for the best claret, or new feather beds or, almost, anything. And he will keep calling me Miss Lydia.

It is very sad here, with no-one to talk to and London such a way off. That is why we have decided to go to Garthdale for a while. At least there we will have Mr and Mrs Hurst to amuse us, and there can be no arguments about who is in charge when Jane and Bingley are away, since Mr Hurst is only an employee.

I am surprised you did not ask me to come with you on your trip. I have lived in foreign parts, after all, and know how to manage natives. It must be terribly boring for you without me to keep you company, for I expect Papa will be poring over his old books all the time and Jane and Bingley will be clambering over old ruins while Margaret Morland does nothing but copy Old Masters. Doctor Morland I do not count on at all for conversation. He always makes me feel as if he is secretly diagnosing something, and will write a prescription before he leaves me.

I should have happily come with you, had I been asked, even though Wyckham has refused flatly to set foot overseas again except as the governor of a colony. Poor soul, I think the Antipodes and the Ionian Islands have made him tired of playing second fiddle. You would think Darcy would do something for him now that he is in parliament, but he ignores me every time I write to him, and Wyckham will not approach him in person. Men are such idle creatures, are they not?

But, seriously, how do you pass your time, surrounded by people who cannot speak a word of a Christian language? But I forget; you have your Marchesa. How very grand that sounds, 'my friend the marchioness'. You will be too grand yourself by now to spare a thought for the wife of a mere knight, I dare say.

There is much more I could say, but I must close now, for Wyckham is come to take me to the theatre in Buxton while it is still convenient. At Garthdale we will have York on our doorstep, too, which, if not quite London, is at least an improvement on Derbyshire.

Even so, to change it for Rome would be so gratifying to

Your loving daughter,

Lydia Wyckham.

Chapter Thirty: Mrs Bennet to Lady Wyckham – The advantages of a masked ball.

Rome

18 January 1837

Dear, dear Lydia,

I am not grand at all, and would never be too grand to forget my favourite daughter. How can you call me grand? It is true that I mix with nobility here daily, but merely being English is enough for that in Italy. All English people are 'Milord this,' and 'Milady that', and are expected to be well off and generous, or, as your father puts it 'rich and foolish.'

A day does not pass but that I wish you were here. Then we would show them a true English Milady, one who cannot be demoted to a mere Signora on the slightest whim. But something may yet be done about that, as I shall tell you.

The Marchesa invited me to a masked ball just last night. This is the first time any of the Roman nobility have recognised us. You will say that I am far too old to enjoy a ball, but I tell you I shall never be too old, not for a proper ball, that is, a society ball, in a real palazzo, with genuine nobility in attendance.

Your father scoffed, of course, but raised no objections. Even he cannot object too strenuously to a Marchesa for a chaperone. She came to the inn to collect me on the evening, and it was then that I began to have my doubts about the evening.

I had my mask, of course, a plain black one, such as we see MacHeath wear on the stage. That was *de rigeur*, but the Marchesa was dressed up in the full costume of a lady of the Ancien Régime, complete with fan and patches. Her mask covered all her face, except for the mouth and chin, and was moulded and painted to resemble a beautiful young lady. In fact, I did not recognise her until she removed it.

"Oh!" I said, "I had not realised that this was a fancy dress ball. I just put on my best gown I brought with me from home."

"Oh, my dear," she replied, "I thought you knew. But come, let me look at you. How charmingly rustic! Surely *mi sei scherzando*, you are joking me. Add a straw hat and you are the perfect *contadina*, no? How you say, peasant girl. You need only a *bastone da pastore*, a, 'ow you say, a shepherd's crook to be the *pastorella*, the shepherdess. You have not one, I suppose? No matter, I know where we can pick one up on the way. Come, *carina*, the caariage waits."

So she whisked me off to the Palazzo Qualcosa (at least, I think that was its name), where my adventures truly began. The coach ride was fairly short, just along to the hill they call the Pincho or something very like, but I was more than a little surprised by the fare.

"Ah," said the Marchesa, when I objected. "I came out without my purse, so I could not pay him for the long trip from my poor lodgings to your apartamento in such a fashionable district. You will not begrudge me, will you, Milady?"

The Marchesa seems to be very prone to forgetting her purse, but she is such good company, and such a very good friend that it is impossible to be annoyed with her.

Well, we entered, gave our cloaks to the footman and proceeded to the ballroom. No sooner had we entered, however, than my friend was addressed by a tall gentleman, very smartly dressed, in a very elaborate costume. They spoke for a few moments in Italian so rapid that I doubt even Mr Bennet or Mrs Morland could have understood what they were saying.

I caught my own name, however, and the gentleman turned to me and bowed.

"You have not met my cousin Mario," the Marchesa said. "Let me introduce you to him now."

Another bow, and a bob on my side.

"Gran piacere, Milady," he intoned, bending to kiss my hand, and then held his own out, as if expecting a kiss in return.

This was far too Italian for me, but one must be polite.

"I am honoured to meet you, sir," I replied. "May I compliment you on your splendid costume? Are you come as the Doge of Venice, with that strange hat and the scarlet robes?"

"I am come as myself, madam," he replied, in English this time, "and these robes are not fancy dress, but my working clothes, for I am the Cardinal Archbishop of Otranto, and, if you will excuse me, I must have a few words with my cousin in private. Permit me to secure a chair for you."

And he swept the Marchesa through a door to one side, pausing only to whisper in the ear of a servant, who instantly disappeared, to return less than a minute later with a fauteuil and a small table which he set by my side, before departing again, to return with a glass of champagne and one of the sticky cakes that Italians are so fond of.

He had scarcely departed again before I found myself addressed by a strikingly handsome and very smartly dressed young man wearing a mask of a fox's face, who bowed, saying –

"Milady Bennet? You will not remember me, but we met at the Aldobrandinis'. I am Antonio Giuliano Carlo Maria dei Barberini di Posca? You know my aunt, the Marchesa?"

"Oh, Count Posca! I remember you very well, my lord. You were so kind as to pick up the handkerchief I dropped on the stairs."

"And you were so kind as to permit me to find you a seat when we got to the ballroom. But what is this 'my lord'? We shall be 'my lording' and 'miladying' each other all night if we continue like this. Call me 'Tonio'. Everyone does. Or 'Count' ,if you cannot bring yourself to be so familiar."

"Oh! Your lordship, that is to say, Count, I could not possibly address you by your Christian name, and still less by a diminutive. What would people say?"

"Very little, I expect. As I told you, everyone calls me 'Tonio'. But here comes my aunt from her conference with that old spider the Cardinal. Come, we must quiz her about it."

"I am not sure what you mean by that, Count Posca. For I assume you do mean something, and are not just saying whatever comes into your head."

"Have I got it wrong? Is not 'quiz' the English word for annoying someone by asking them questions about their failings?"

"It is a word I am not accustomed to use, Count, nor to hear it used, especially about one's elders. I am a lady of a certain age, and find it congenial to stick to the customs of my youth."

"But that cannot be so very long ago, *mia bella donna*. I cannot believe it was very long ago."

"You must not 'quiz' a lady about her age, Count. That is another thing that is not done in England. I have ten grandchildren, one of them married, and half the others full grown."

"Then you must have been, 'ow you say, a child bride. The word of an English lady is not to be disputed, but you ask me to believe something which my eyes deny."

It took me a little while to work this out as a compliment, but when I did, you may be sure, Lydia, dear, that I was inclined to smile upon the Count thenceforth.

His announcing to his aunt, when she joined us, that I was engaged to him for the first two sets did nothing to lessen that inclination, you may be sure. Nor did his refusal to leave my side for the rest of the evening, nor his insistence an escorting me to our lodgings before going on with his aunt to theirs.

A masked ball is one thing, where one's face is hidden, and any persona at all may be adopted, but daily life is quite another, and it was a genuine surprise when he turned up to breakfast the following morning along with the Marchesa.

Since then, however, we have become fast friends. There can be nothing in it, I am sure. I am a happily married woman, and he knows it, but there is something that makes the attention of such a handsome and well-bred young man awaken feelings long forgotten in the female breast.

Do not tease me, Lydia darling, but in his presence I feel thirty years younger, and valued more than your father ever did. He must have noticed by now that I am out with the Count every day, while he pores over his books and grubs over his holes in the ground.

Do not tease me, I beg. Surely I may have a little, innocent fun while your father pursues his own interests? If only I had you here with me, it would be different. What fun we should have together, and how happy it would make

Your gratified and confused mother,

J. Bennet.

P.S.

Tonio says he has friends in the Papal chancellery who could make you father a Barone or a Conte for the appropriate contribution to charity. Imagine that; Countess Bennet would really put Lady Lucas in her place.

Chapter Thirty-one : Mr Bennet to Mrs Darcy – Definitely not a Cicisbeo

Viale del Pincio

19 January 1837

Dear Lizzie,

Calm your fears, my love. Count Posca is definitely not your mother's *cicisbeo*. I make no doubt he would be if he could. In fact, I am sure he is out for whatever he can get. Rome is full of such characters, even more so than Florence. He was introduced to us by Marchesa Cacciasoldi who is a sort of professional hanger-on who frequents all the English parties without anyone ever seeming to know who first introduced her into that circle. I rather suspect she inherited the position from her mother, Roman society being so lax, quite the opposite of what one would expect from the capital of the Catholic faith. Although, when one considers the history of the Popes – of the entire College of Cardinals, even – I suppose it is exactly what one should expect. One need only mention the Borgias.

But I digress. The young Count (yes, he is young, and handsome, and agreeable, and penniless, as are most of the Roman nobility) makes himself agreeable to all of us and to your mother in particular. To do so is evidently his profession, and he makes no bones about it. He has been useful in keeping your mother amused and entertained and in good spirits during my illness, and even more useful in continuing in those duties now that I am up and about again.

Never for a moment think that I do not know what he would be at. None of us – except your mother, I believe – have any doubts about that. Indeed, we held a family conference about it not long since.

It was Bingley who first brought into the open what we had all been thinking for weeks when, shortly after the young man had departed with your mother on his arm to attend the opera, he announced –

"I dare say you will all tell me I am wrong – you usually do – but I do not think that young man is quite the thing. I do not like the appearance of how he is constantly flapping around Mrs Bennet. I am sure he is out to take advantage."

"Surely not?" responded Jane, "He is a count, after all."

"And what difference does that make?" Margaret enquired. "Besides, there is an old Italian proverb I remember from our days on Lake Como that goes *'In Italia ognuno è Conte di Nulla'*. 'In Italy, everyone is count of nothing'. I am very glad that Charles has raised the subject at last, for I, too, am uneasy about *il Signor Conte*."

"I have to say that I agree with Margaret," the Doctor agreed, "since we are always in perfect accord, but I think we must ask what you think, Mr Bennet. It is you who are most closely concerned, after all."

"It is true that there are more counts than one can shake a stick at in Italy," I replied, "and even more than that in Rome itself, and I doubt very much if the young man can trace his ancestry back to the Scipios, or even the Anicians. I understand your doubts, your suspicions, which I know quite well are of the Count only. I share them, as far as the young man goes, but I have no notion of his being successful in any designs he may have on Mrs Bennet.

You say he will take advantage. I say 'let him try'. What can he achieve? He is after money, you say. I dare say he is. But how much can he extract from Mrs Bennet, who has only her allowance to squander on him? And if it gives her pleasure to do so, who am I to object?"

"Forgive me, Mr Bennet, but it is not just the money we care about," said Bingley. "It is not even mostly the money we care about. It is Mrs Bennet's reputation, and the distress she may find herself in. We all know this person will leave her as soon as he has got as much as he thinks he is going to get."

"We do. I do, certainly, and I think Mrs Bennet does, too, if she has thought about it at all. As for her reputation, how can that be harmed by acting as every other married lady in Rome acts? As for anything that might truly harm that reputation, can you imagine the reception the poor lad would meet with should he attempt anything improper? Mrs Bennet would not understand him for a month of Sundays, and if understanding were to be forced upon her, she would instantly brain *il Signor Conte* with the nearest convenient piece of statuary. In the meantime, he amuses her, he gives her pleasure, and he performs a useful service for the rest of us. I have been married far longer than any of you, my dears, and you may take my word for it. If *il signor Contino vuol' ballare*, it will be to my tune."

So there you have it, my Lizzie. My thoughts on the subject have not changed significantly since then, even though I have now had the advantage of viewing the bills for the toys and trinkets your mother bought for the young man in the last month on my credit. She has always loved spending my money, and went for too long with too little of it to spend. Let her enjoy it while she can.

And I will enjoy it too, for writing this letter has clarified my thoughts on the Count's offer to show me his subterranean delights. I will take him up on it. Who knows, the time spent might even turn out not to be wasted, and it will make a change from sitting around in a sheet.

Next time I may have discoveries to relate that will make my name among scholars at last. Until then, be of good cheer, my darling daughter, as is

Your doting father,

F. Bennet.

Chapter Thirty-two : Mr Bennet to Mrs Darcy – The Perils of Painting

Viale del Pincio
25 January 1837

Dear Lizzie,

I have decided that I must write more often, since you appear to be so concerned about our little doings here. This reminds me that I have myself failed to express any curiosity about your own affairs. How is Darcy faring in his new seat? Is he Prime Minister yet? I assume as a matter of course that he won his election, but there are no regular newspapers here, and we must rely on newly-arriving travellers for intelligence from home.

You will already be wondering at this change in me. I sometimes wonder myself.

My new career as an artist's model will soon be over, it seems. Margaret tells me that she will soon have no more need of my services, and no modern Raphael has so far appeared to be desirous of them. It is, perhaps, just as well. We were becoming far too easy with each other after the awkwardness of the first few sessions, and I confess I have looked at her in quite a different way since I caught Count Posca kissing your mother on the stairs the other night. Much more enforced intimacy might not be the best of ideas.

The *capolavoro* is progressing well, she tells me, while thwarting all attempts at getting a sight of it. Pericles needs but a few more touches and he will be ready. The problem now is Aspasia, for whom we are sadly short of a model. Your mother did suggest that, if I could be Pericles, she did not see why she should not be Aspasia, but when informed of the costume Margaret had in mind she very soon withdrew her offer.

Aspasia, you see, is to be clothed very much in the Grecian style, her Ionic chiton in the sheerest material, with one side slipping from her shoulder to reveal her profession. She is also to be much younger than Pericles. Margaret is very much against engaging a professional for her model, as the typical Roman figure is not what she is looking for. I think we all agree that introducing an outsider into our household is to be avoided if possible.

But that leaves us still with our dilemma. Jane will not hear of it, of course. I forget precisely who suggested her, but she was instantly denying the possibility, all blushes and stammers, Miss Anna Coluthon herself.

"Me!" she cried, sitting down again with a most frightened look. "Indeed you must excuse me. I could not pose for anything if you were to give me the world. No, indeed, I cannot pose."

Bingley thought it rather a good idea, but to no avail.

"No, indeed, Mr. Bingley, you must excuse me. You cannot have an idea. It would be absolutely impossible for me. If I were to undertake it, I should only disappoint you."

It shows how agitated she was that she said Mr Bingley, and not Charles. How often have you heard her refer to her husband thus?

Your mother, having refused the position herself, appeared to be rather inclined to secure it for her daughter.

"What a piece of work here is about nothing," she said. "I am quite ashamed of you, Jane, to make such a difficulty of obliging your father and our friends in a trifle of this sort—so kind as they are to you! Take the part with a good grace, and let us hear no more of the matter, I entreat. You have always been so beautiful, and I long to see that beauty properly commemorated."

"You must excuse me, indeed you must excuse me," cried Jane, growing more and more red from excessive agitation, and looking distressfully at me.

"Do not urge her, madam," I interposed, for the poor girl was becoming quite distressed, and I was become sorry I had ever mentioned the matter. "It is not fair to urge her in this manner. You see she does not like to pose. Let her choose for herself, as well as the rest of us. Her judgment may be quite as safely trusted. Do not urge her any more."

"Well" said your mother, "I do not know what we are to do then."

"We are to go on as before," I replied, "in peace and harmony."

"Certainly we must," seconded Margaret. "These problems have a way of arranging themselves, and I should not dream of putting dear Jane to such trouble. Indeed, I am sorry that she has been put to this much."

So you see with what earth-shattering problems we divert ourselves here. I have an idea for that particular problem myself, but will discuss it with Margaret first, at our next session, which will also, probably, be our last.

Once that is out of the way, I shall be sure to avail myself of the Count's offer of guidance to the subterranean mysteries of the Eternal City, and equally sure of taking up as much of his time in doing so as I can.

What the result of these efforts may be, I shall relate in my next.

Until then, be sure that you are never far from the thoughts of

Your loving father,

F. Bennet.

Chapter Thirty-three : Mr Bennet to Mrs Darcy - Grotesque Discoveries

Viale del Pincio
4 February 1837

My dear Lizzie,

I have seen wonders. I have walked in a Caesar's palace, and viewed the paintings on his walls and ceilings. I am speechless with wonder at them. I have made a discovery that is at the same time tremendously moving and utterly frustrating.

How did this come about? Let me tell you.

Picture your dear old father clambering up a narrow street on a steep hill on the south side of Rome, with your mother's favourite Italian count by his side. The neighbourhood is, shall we say, not the very best in Rome, and the ground underfoot not the cleanest. Every now and then an upper story window is opened and a bucketful of material I would call dubious were it not that there can be no doubt about it is thrown out to add to the general gaiety.

How did these circumstances come about? Through my own obstinate persistence. *Otium, Catulle, tibi molestumst* says Catullus, and he knew what he was talking about. Since I have been banned from further participation in Margaret's new painting, time has hung heavy on my hands. It has not helped that such a veil of secrecy is now drawn across further progress of the picture, which, I must confess, I was rather looking forward to seeing in its finished state. None of us is entirely free from vanity. Our omniscient physician has declared the daily sun baths no longer needed, so I have no excuse for demanding a place on the terrace, purely by coincidence, at the same time as the daily sittings.

Perhaps it is because I am actually feeling so much better than when we came here that I feel the urge to busy myself in something more physically active than poring through manuscripts and incunabula. At any rate, I finally challenged *Signor Contino* on his promise of secret caverns filled with treasure, and thus it was that I was led to this far from prepossessing quarter, downriver from all our old haunts, near to the old port of Rome.

The street, or rather alley in front of us twisted and turned so that it was impossible to keep one's bearings, and I should have sworn that we passed the same corner several times. Eventually we stopped outside a tavern, of sorts, with a couple of tables outside, practically blocking the gangway.

"*Beppo è qui giu?*" enquired my guide. The grunt he received for a reply appeared to satisfy him, for he led the way into a smoky, dimly-lit room where the smell of unwashed bodies almost drowned the stink of tobacco.

"*Beppo, carino!*" he addressed the most disreputable looking of the four burly villains playing some unknown card game at a corner table.

There followed a burst of dialect so thick and so rapid that I could follow less than one word in three, at the end of which Posca turned to me.

"Beppo here knows all about these caverns," he said. "I have told him you wish to see one of them, and he has agreed to conduct you. I will leave you in his hands, for I must not be observed taking part in such doings."

"Wait a minute," I replied. "You are going now, and I am to trust this... this person to be my guide? Who knows but that I will never be seen again?"

"*Non preoccuparsi, Signor Bennet.* You will be perfectly safe with Beppo. I assure you, on the honour of a Posca. Besides, he knows I will find him if anything happens to you."

And with that, he was gone, before I could move to stop him.

I was not best pleased, as you may gather, my dear. There I was, alone in an unknown part of Rome and a quandary. I could trust Count Posca and his...acquaintance, or I could trust myself to find my way back to civilisation.

My doubt was resolved by Beppo's outstretched hand and his demands for

"*Soldi.*"

If I was merely to be robbed and dumped down some back alley, why should he be demanding money now? If that was what he was about to do, he would have it all, soon enough. In any case, it was clear that there would be no leaving this place until money had changed hands.

I had one of the new half-sovereigns in my pocket ready for just such an eventuality. I have never been able to think of these new coins as real money, not like the old guineas. They may be easier to reckon in, but they are not as satisfying.

The sight of gold made all the difference, however, and he instantly led the way out. Into more back alleys, even narrower and twistier than before, to an even more disreputable looking inn, where he introduced me to another person, also called Beppo, who led me to a third, and so on, until, at last, a friend of a friend of a friend consented to show me what I was looking for.

Finding myself thus abandoned with yet another stranger, I decided to assert myself a little.

"Lasciami dovinare," I said *"Mi serve chiamarti Beppo."*[5]

"Si, signor," he replied

"Perque quello non è il tuo nome[6]?" I continued.

"Esatto!" he replied, with a grin that revealed his execrable teeth.

"Ma il Signore Inglese parla Italiano?"[7] he continued.

"Nessuna parola," I replied, *"Ti stai sbagliando. D'ora in poi parlo solo inglese."*[8]

He looked dubious, but complied.

"Come wiz me," he beckoned, and I followed.

By now I was beginning to regret starting so high with my largesse and my supply of half-sovereigns was running short. More fool me for not starting with a crown, or even a half-crown, but I had no notion when the Count left me that I should be expected to tip half the rascals of the

---

[5] Let me guess. I must call you 'Beppo'.
[6] Because that is not your name?
[7] But the English gentleman speaks Italian?
[8] Not a word. You deceive youself. From now on I speak only English.

Romagna. My final guide led me to the foot of Monte Testaccio, by design, I am sure, and I thought I could see where this was leading. To be sure, I might be completely wrong, but if I was to have my throat slit and my purse with it, there had been ample opportunity already, and, moreover, I recognised the colonnade towards which we were heading.

The panel in the wall to which he led me was no great surprise. We had already visited this end of town, and I had read and heard enough descriptions of this custom to know the ordeal I must now face. It showed a human face, surrounded by a mane of hair, with mouth gaping liking an ancient theatrical mask.

"*Ecco la bocca della verità,*" my guide announced. He paused and appeared to be mumbling to himself.

"The mouth of the Truth," he continued. "Before I take you where you want to go, you must swear never to betray the secret. You must put your hand in the mouth of the truth and swear it. If you swear false, the mouth will bite your hand off."

I was already familiar with this superstition, and had meant to get round to testing its inspiration. There are so many things to see and do in Rome, however. I believed in it even less than I believed in fairies, and was perfectly willing to undergo the test to convince my companion of my sincerity.

So I held up my right hand and thrust my left one into the gaping mouth.

"*Lo giuro.*" I said.

For a moment, seeing the avid expectancy on my guide's face, I almost felt as if the stone were closing in on my fingers, and was quite relieved, in a way, to see my hand, whole and unblemished, when I withdrew it.

'Beppo' sighed. His relief was evident.

"*Buonissimo!*" he exclaimed. "Now I show you the buried palazzo."

I will not burden you, my dear, with a long description of more twisting alleyways through which he led me, nor attempt even to guess the general direction of our travels, but we eventually arrived somewhere I could speak for, for the hulking mass of the Colosseum could be seen to our left, towering over the hovels that surrounded it.

"Now you meet my friend Beppo," said my Beppo. I might have known I had not yet run the gamut of the Beppos.

This one was different, however. Instead of demanding money and leading me to yet another intermediary, after a short, impenetrable, dialogue between the two, he beckoned me inside. Arming himself with a crowbar, he led me through his house (which only my being his guest prevents me from calling a hovel) to his back garden, or rather, yard. My Beppo followed along.

I can see my narration is suffering from a surfeit of Beppos. For clarity in future I will refer to 'my' Beppo as 'Beppone', that is to say 'Big Beppo', and the final Beppo as 'Beppino', 'Little Beppo.' Whether this will help remains to be seen.

We stood around for a few moments while they looked at me expectantly.

"Well? I had to say, at last, "Where is it?"

"*Eccola!*" replied Beppone, with a vague gesture towards a corner of the yard, "*La porta degli Inferi.*"

Beppino said nothing, but made use of his crowbar to move the great slab of stone that adorned the said corner, revealing a dark hole, barely wider than my shoulders.

"*Eccola!*" he repeated.

Peering down the hole revealed nothing but darkness, endless darkness, as far as I could see. It was rather deep.

"And how am I to get down there?" I enquired. "Is there a ladder?"

"No, no ladder. *Fune.*"

"I am expected to scramble down a rope? And up again? You have wasted my time, Signori, and may forget about wasting any more."

"What you mean, 'scramble'? 'Scramble' is cooking eggs. *Come c'entrano le uova?*"[9]

"Am I to climb down your rope, then? I decline. I am an old man."

"No climb. We tie rope. We... *Come si dice 'le facemo scendere' in Inglese?*"

"You will lower me down? Then how am I to get up again?"

"We pull."

"And how am I to find my way down there? Are there signposts? Is there a marked route? Are there lights?"

---

[9] What have eggs got to do with it?

"*Cosa ha detto?* I come. I show."

This last from Big Beppo.

I confess that visions of lying at the bottom of the hole with my throat slit and my pockets emptied made yet another appearance in my mind at this point. But, my former reasoning was still sound, and the premise unchanged. If such were their end, they had neglected many such opportunities already. True, there had been no convenient hole before, but there had been the equally convenient river to dispose of the evidence.

It was curiosity, in the end, that made me agree. And cupidity, of course, for fame, rather than money. If there were truly relics of the ancient past below the surface here, then I wanted to be their discoverer. Such lectures I should give! Such papers I should write! How Casaubon and Potts and Collins and the entire Senior Common Room of my old college would repine!

So I permitted myself to be swathed in coils of rather dubious rope and lowered, dangling, into the abyss, where I stood shamefacedly at the bottom, feeling seven kinds of fool, until Beppone came down to release me.

"I should have thought your smaller friend more apt for tunnelling beneath the earth," I remarked, convinced that if I were once to show fear it would be the end of me.

"Oh, no," came the reply, as Beppone busied himself with lighting a stub of candle. "He never come down here. He have too much *paura*."

"You said there was nothing to fear."

"There is nothing to fear. Tunnels many years old. Why they come crashing down on our heads now? They say full of ghosts of old Romans, but I never see any. Lots of banditti, is true, but never bother anyone except police. And rich tourists, of course."

The comfort I derived from these words you may well appreciate, my dear, but the nameless dread with which I entered on my explorations with such a Job's comforter as a guide was very soon suppressed by the wonders that I saw.

There is a whole network of tunnels criss-crossing beneath the Aventine hill there, following the lines of ancient streets and corridors, with entire rooms, possibly entire houses opening off them. They are, I believe, as yet unknown to academics, although tomb-robbers and various other opportunists have long since cleared them of anything intrinsically valuable. But what is left is amazing. Such wall paintings, such ceilings, such mosaics! Such statuary, even!

I could write pages more, but this letter is already unconscionably long, and I must digest my discoveries before I can be coherent about them.

Something I *can* be coherent about, I fear, is the continued absence of any news at all from your errant son and his bride. If the Romans had something like the old Bow Street Runners, or the new Metropolitan Police, from whom one may hire a detective officer for one's own ends, I should have set one on their trail long since. The police here, however, are interested only in spying on everyone who is not a priest, foreigners and natives alike, for ever-present fear of revolution.

Looking back over my scrawl, I see that I have now omitted to describe, or even enumerate the great discoveries I promised you.

I can only apologise and excuse myself. The truth is, I have not taken them all in and got them straight in my own mind as yet.

Bear with me, my love, and I shall yet relate great things, both of the honeymooners and of my discoveries.

Until then, you may congratulate your loving and serendipitous father,

F. Bennet.

Chapter Thirty-four : Mr Bennet to Mrs Darcy : Subterranean Ramblings

Viale del Pincio

24 February 1837

Dear Lizzie,

Pray forgive the lateness of this epistle. I have been very, very busy. Not alone neither, for I believe we have all been very busy, each in his or her peculiar way.

Jane and Bingley are taking their duties as tourists very seriously, and are determined to leave no ruin unscrambled over and no artistic masterpiece unogled. The weather has been their friend, for February in Rome is like May in Meryton, or July in Derbyshire.

James Morland is in great demand among the physical community, not only in Rome but in Bologna and Florence and even as far afield as Milan and Naples. He is constantly riding about the place to give lectures, demonstrations and even second opinions. We tend to forget what a treasure we have at Meryton.

Margaret has her *magnum opus*, of course, although she is currently at a stand for want of a model for Aspasia. There is no shortage of professional models in Rome, but none of them so far have fitted her requirements. They all look too Italian, apparently, and form too great a contrast with her Pericles. I am not sure whether to take that as a compliment or no.

Your mother has her Italian swain in attendance every day, and every day she allows herself to be taken to some new entertainment, some new garden, some new *casa particolare* only open to friends of the owners, and she has amassed a rather unlikely number of souvenirs of her visits. If she is determined to take them all home I fear we may have to buy a new trunk.

My own subterranean wanderings *col Gran Beppone* have very soon become almost as frustrating as they are enlightening. Every day has brought more revelations about Roman painting, Roman life and Roman interiors. Do not misunderstand me, however, my dear. This is no underground Pompei of which I talk, but, even so, amazing to the true scholar. But there is a problem. I cannot adequately describe my discoveries in words only, and pictures have proven beyond my abilities.

My own attempts at sketches, with the best will in the world, can only be described as pitiful. I am sure the Beppos would co-operate in the removal of choice pieces, for the right money. Yet, somehow, I cannot bring myself to chisel pieces of plaster off walls where they have lain undisturbed for nearly two thousand years, purely for the satisfaction of taking them home with me and writing a learned monograph.

'Why are you worrying about making sketches of paintings on old walls?' I hear you asking. "Have you forgotten that you have an esteemed painter, an almost-Royal-Academician in your party?'

I have not forgotten, my pet, but I am reluctant to ask Margaret for help. She is grown peevish since her work on Pericles has come to a stand, and grows every day more so at her inability to find a suitable Aspasia. I can hardly go up to her and say 'Well, you have nothing better to do without a new model, so you might as well do some drawings for me,' can I?

I wish we had Mr Fox Talbot here with us, with his magic boxes to take some of his light drawings for us. The examples he gave to the Morlands when they visited him last summer are amazing, perfect images created purely by the action of light on his treated paper.

I might as well wish for Raphael himself, who dangled from the same rope and copied the same decorations as I have, if we are to believe the tales my Roman guides tell me.

Perhaps if I were to take lots of lamps and some tracing paper?

Forgive me, my dear, for boring you with my problems when what you want to hear is news, preferably of Frank and Mina. I should be very glad to pass on such news, if we had any. I suppose it is too much to hope that young Frank may have written a few words to his mother recently?

You may be sure that anything we chance to hear will be passed on instantly by

Your loving father,

F. Bennet.

Chapter Thirty-five: Mrs Darcy to Mr Bennet – Stating the obvious

London

12 March 1837

Dear Papa,

You are the cleverest person I know, but sometimes you are so clever that you miss what seems obvious to us ordinary mortals.

You are interested in your discoveries from a historical point of view, because of what they tell you about Roman life all those years ago. That is your interest because you are a scholar, and a classicist. But there are other interests to be considered, you know. Do you seriously think that Margaret would not be interested in seeing these examples of ancient art? Or that she would be loath to view paintings which inspired Raphael himself?

I rather think she would be disappointed if she were not offered the opportunity of seeing these things with her own eyes, and I suspect that, once seen, you would be hard put to stop her making copies.

My advice is 'try her, and see'. I do not think you will regret it.

You will think me a terrible Philistine if I admit that I am less concerned about these antique Romans than I am about a modern one, namely Mama's 'young man'. I cannot help but wonder if setting you a-grubbing in the bowels of the earth might not suit your Count Posca very well, since while you are marvelling at your ancient images you are less well placed to impede his own machinations.

Perhaps I am wrong, but, from what you tell me, I can see only mercenary reasons why he should be prepared to devote so much of his time to a married lady of a certain age with an apparently complaisant husband. I ought to add that, from what Mama tells me in her letters, and from what Lydia tells me of the letters she has received from Mama, I see no reason to doubt what I assume to be the case.

Quite the contrary, in fact. Mama's letters to Lydia are written in quite a different tone to the one she uses to me, and contain much more information of her relations with the young count. All this was meant to be confidential, of course, but one might as well have the Town Crier proclaim it at the crossroads as entrust a secret to Lydia. I am not as who should say alarmed, not yet, but I cannot help but wonder.

I will say no more at the moment, but I will quote from our favourite opera.

'*Figaro, alerta! Figaro, alerta!*'

The honeymoon couple are still, alas, incommunicado, and yet we have proof in the form of a name scratched on a desk in the schoolroom that at least one of them *can* write.

If they ever remember, it will certainly relieve one fear of

Your concerned daughter,

Elizabeth Darcy.

Chapter Thirty-six: Mr Bennet to Mrs Darcy - Recording History

Viale del Pincio
24 March 1837

Dear Lizzie,

You were right about Margaret, I confess, although she was not to be press-ganged into helping me, but held out for an acceptable Aspasia in exchange.

This was something to which I had already devoted much thought, and a few words with Arianna very soon answered the purpose. I knew Margaret had not asked her out of delicate feelings towards all concerned.

Arianna was, after all, Mrs Bennet's servant rather than the Morlands' and had taken upon herself the charge of the entire party out of mere goodwill, and, I believe, some little delight in having a couple of Italian underlings to boss about.

Her reluctance to perform for Madama Margaret was not entirely convincing. She considers *ta eikona tis Despoinis Margaritis*[10] as little short of miraculous, and I could see that the thought of appearing in one was tempting.

Our conversation was revealing. How little one thinks about servants! They are there, they perform their functions, and they are paid for it. That is the sum of their existence, as far as most masters are concerned, and even the most

---

[10] The images of Madam Margaret

conscientious employers never think of their servants as being possessed of private lives.

It had never occurred to me that Arianna might have ambitions to return home to Corfu, nor that she had been in correspondence with her family all this time. More than that, she still harboured hopes of marriage and children of her own, and her parents had found a suitable young man for her, of good Corfiote family and an ample estate, and were urging her to return.

All this was news indeed, and I reflected that it had never even occurred to me that Arianna could read and write, although that must be the case as she had been employed by the Wyckhams not merely as a nursemaid but as a sort of cut-price governess for their children.

All this came out almost as soon as I took her aside for a conversation which she took to be foreshadowing her dismissal, and must explain her reasons for wishing to stay with us a little longer. Her dowry was not quite complete. She had been saving ever since she came to England. While she was working for '*Il Generale e milady Wyckham*' this had not always been easy. Since we had made up her arrears of pay, however, when we engaged her after Wyckham had turned her off, the case was altered. What with her pay and her tips, she was now but ten guineas short of the goal of a hundred guineas which she had set for herself. A hundred guineas might not seem a good foundation for life to you or I, my dear Lizzie, but I assure you that in Corfu it will go further than a thousand would in England. Similarly, ten guineas may not seem much of a hindrance to you or I, but to a servant it may represent several years' pay.

Arianna represented herself as unworthy to appear in one of Madama Margaret's miraculous icons, especially in the same one as Signor Bennet, but I could see that her vanity was piqued. I chanced to have in my pocket an Austrian four ducat piece, a gold coin the size of an English crown, and hugely impressive. The sight of this marvel, and the promise of its payment for services rendered as a model for Pericles' companion worked wonders. I doubt the poor girl had ever seen so much gold in one piece in her lifetime. And yet, the four ducat piece, though fine and large, is very thin in proportion, and worth only about two guineas, which I am willing to wager would not have had the same effect at all.

It was Margaret who then needed more coaxing. Arianna would be satisfactory for the figure she had in mind, but her face was 'all wrong, not what she had in mind'.

Why this should be so in the case of a raven-haired Mediterranean beauty and a genuine Greek to boot, she declined to specify exactly, although she was, apparently, too young. I have no idea what age Aspasia was when the Peloponnesian Wars broke out, nor any real idea of Arianna's age. She was not yet fifteen when she came back from Corfu with us, and must still be in her twenties.

"Can you not paint the figure meanwhile?" I asked, "and come and see my ancient Roman paintings in your spare time? Who knows, you may find inspiration there."

She hummed and hawed, but I could see her curiosity was piqued, and it was undeniable that no other way had yet presented itself to progress with her masterpiece. Eventually, she agreed to view these 'ancient mysteries' as she called them, and to defer her decision until she had done so.

Even so, we very nearly stalled at the first hurdle. The Beppos were perfectly agreeable to admit a lady to their secret, for an appropriate consideration, but the lady herself refused point blank to be lowered, dangling from a rope, into the murky chasm beneath her feet, holding out at the least for a practicable ladder.

A ladder was at length procured, a very long ladder, which stretched right through Little Beppo's hovel along the corridor into his back yard, and took a great deal of heaving, dragging and shoving to set in place, where it severely restricted the space of the entrance hole.

Personally, I was surprised that a ladder of such length could be found, for it had seemed an age to reach the bottom, at an unplumbable depth while I had swung from their rope like an oversize pendulum.

In fact, I suppose the first corridor tunnel was little further down than the height of a two-story house, and the walk from there to the first wall paintings took but a few moments.

The moment Margaret saw the first set, I knew we had her. She grabbed the candle from Beppone and held it to the wall, peering closely at the scene before her.

"To tell the truth," she said, "I had heard that marvellous paintings had been discovered in tunnels in the side of a Roman hill some three hundred years ago, and inspired the use of the grotesque in art that had previously been purely classical. But I had also heard that Raphael, Michelangelo and others had deliberately destroyed everything they found, so that no-one else could copy them. Yet, there is something here. You are right, Mr Bennet, there is definitely something here. The perspective is not right, and yet, it is not wrong, neither, but… different. More light! I must have more light. I will make some sketches, but the light is so bad."

"You might do better to contain your patience," I suggested. "These are far from the best examples available. Come, Beppone will show us around, and we may come back tomorrow with a whole bunch of candles."

"Better still," she replied, "I am sure one of James's doctor friends has one of those new Argand lamps, and can be persuaded to part with it for a while. With that, and a few candles and mirrors, I hope to do justice to your finds, Mr Bennet."

And so she has, Lizzie, my dear, and you would be astonished to see her sketches, and even more astonished to see the watercolours she has made from them. When we get home, I shall have engravings made, and with them I shall publish such monographs, such volumes!

I have never, as you know, cared much for neither fame nor money, but I fear I may soon have to put up with both, for I have developed a theory. Tacitus writes about the great *Domus Aurea* of Nero, that ridiculous emperor's ridiculously large and extravagantly decorated palace on the Palatine hill. Later on, the emperor Titus is known to have incurred expenses for repairs to the *Domus Aurea* on the *Esquiline* hill. Whether Nero's folly, with its three hundred public rooms and no bedrooms was on the Palatine or the Esquiline is a subject which has exercised scholars ever since.

Judging from the glimpse of the Colosseum I had on my first underground exploration, and further glimpses of known landmarks since then, I believe the hole down which I was lowered is situated just where the Palatine merges into the Esquiline, and that I have been walking in the footsteps of Nero, in his palace that was so huge that it stretched over both hills, and in the process began the gentrification of the Esquiline, which had been a slum until then, and has returned to that state since.

I have already set pen to paper with my thesis, but no real progress may be made without the engravings for my plates, which must wait until we return to England, for I would not dream of entrusting such a task to a Roman artificer.

Now that my health is fully restored (James Morland might not agree, but physicians will always quibble) the only thing holding back our return is the continued absence of Frank and Mina. They have not turned up at home by some circuitous route, by any chance?

I suppose not, and I suppose we shall have to continue our enquiries.

By the way, please note the address above. Your last few missives have been forwarded from our old inn. It is not like you to forget that we have moved to a more salubrious, if less convenient part of Rome in preparation for the summer heat.

The best preparation we could possibly make would be to forsake Italy altogether and come home, but I dare say we shall have to linger a little while longer. Rome, fortunately, is a city that contains something for everyone. I have my discoveries, your mother has her young man,

Margaret her painting of both genres, and Morland his consultations, and, indeed, demonstrations, for he is much sought after among the physical fraternity here, who suffer under so many Papal restrictions. I should worry about Jane and Bingley, but they are both so placid, each of them so complying, that nothing may ever be resolved on; so easy, that every *cicerone* will cheat them; and so generous, that they will always exceed their income in the service of others.

I hope, in preventing the last, at least to be of some service to them, and meanwhile they seem happy enough viewing ruins and gardens and mixing with English emigrés and Papal nobility alike.

Yet all good things must come to an end, and unless the errant honeymooners come to light soon we must leave them to their Italian devices.

You are the most sensible and discerning of my daughters, and you are Frank's mother to boot. Can you not think of anywhere he may have mentioned an inclination to visit that we have not tried?

Strike that enquiry out, my dear. I know you would have said so if you could. It is merely the ruminating aloud of

Your loving and regrettably impatient father,

F. Bennet.

Chapter Thirty-seven : Mr Bennet to Mrs Darcy – An Unexpected Obstacle

Rome

1 April 1837

Dear Lizzie,

I am sending this via one of Pennworth's friends, since I have reason to believe our post is being read by the Papal authorities.

Yes, ridiculous as it seems, your father is under investigation as an agitator or some sort of secret plotter. How this came about, I do not know.

How I came to know of it is easily told, however. I was browsing in the Forum yesterday when I found myself accosted by two large gentlemen in the uniform of the Swiss Guards. I do not mean Michelangelo's uniform, all doublets and pantaloons and halberds, but in their modern uniform, which is quite as serious as any Continental uniform may be. They also had serious hangers by their sides and eminently serious muskets on their shoulders. These gentlemen requested me to accompany them, and reinforced their request with their muskets when I enquired as to their reason, so that I felt myself obliged to comply.

Margaret was walking with me at the time, and promised to carry this news to the rest of our company and make all efforts to secure my release.

My captors led me through the old centre and across the Tiber via Castel Santangelo, and into a building near the Vatican, where they left me to sit in an empty, almost bare room for some little while, to reflect on all the stories I had heard of *francs juges* and so forth.

Eventually, a young man in clerical robes entered, saying "Monsignor will see you now" and showed me into a larger room, sumptuously furnished, where a much older cleric sat behind a heavy desk.

Motioning me to a low chair in front of the desk, the young priest then sat at a smaller desk to one side, and took up pen and paper, as if about to write.

His superior fixed me with an icy gaze.

"Well, Signor Bennet," he said, "What do you have to say to me?"

I had a great deal to say, as you might expect, and I said it, dropping as many influential names into my discourse as I could think of, but all I had to say was waved aside.

"This is mere bluster," rejoined my interlocutor, "and only to be expected. It will not do. We know all about you, Signor Bennet, and everything you have been up to. I advise you to confess now and save us both a great deal of trouble."

At this point I had no more idea of what he was talking about than you have, Lizzie dear, and I said so.

I confess I have not the faintest idea of what you mean," I replied, "nor under what authority you have had me – I will not say dragged, for I came quietly – summoned here. May I know whom I have the honour to address?"

"My name does not matter. What does matter is that you have been brought here under my authority as an officer of the *Sanctum Officium de Fidei Propaganda.*"

"Good Lord!" I exclaimed. "I did not expect the Spanish Inqusition!"

"No-one expects the Holy Inquisition," he replied. "Amongst our weapons, surprise is by no means the least. But we are not merely Spanish any more, but universal. And you would do well to answer my questions."

"I have answered your questions, sir. What more do you expect me to say?"

"Come, Signor Bennet, you would do well to tell me all you know, to name names. You were seen entering the house of a known *carbonaro*. We know all about your secret meetings with malignants and heretics in caverns beneath the hill to the north of the Colosseum, and of your plot to dethrone his Holiness and install a people's republic."

"Then you know more than I do, sir. And what on earth does a charcoal burner have to do with me? And you would do well to remember sir, that I am an Englishman, and not without friends."

"And, unfortunately, without an official envoy to the Holy See at the moment."

Where things might have progressed from there I have no notion, for at that point a guard entered and whispered in the ear of the young amanuensis, who in turn whispered in his master's ear.

"It appears that you do have friends, Signor Bennet," my interrogator admitted. "You may go now. Father Aidan will show you out. But remember this. I have many eyes, and they are all upon you. I know you now, and you will not escape."

"Well," I thought, "what was all that about?" as I followed the young priest to an anteroom, where I was handed over to a very gorgeously attired cleric, complete with an unusual hat.

"Mr Bennet?" this individual enquired.

"Yes, sir," I replied.

"It is fortunate your lovely daughter and her husband thought to come to me with your letter of introduction from Lord Pennworth," he continued, in perfect and barely accented English. "It was remiss in you not to have presented it sooner, for I could have protected you from such annoyances. But come with me now and I will take you to your family."

"I thank you, sir," I said, as I struggled to remember the direction on the Roman letter of introduction. I had not bothered to follow it up after the disappointment in Florence, you see.

My struggles were ineffectual, and I must ask –

"To whom do I owe this timely service, sir?"

He smiled, and held out his hand. His left hand.

"I am Silvio Aurelio Massimo," he said, "a humble servant of God, and, for my sins, Cardinal Archbishop of Otranto."

Only the way he pronounced Otranto, in the Italian fashion with the stress on the first syllable rather than the second, betrayed that he was not English.

For a moment I was completely nonplussed. Then the light caught the massive amethyst on the third finger of his left hand, and I realised he was waiting for me to kiss his ring.

Although it was the first time I had ever performed such an act, I believe I managed it without discredit. The proprieties thus observed, I was able to remark-

"I had the pleasure of visiting Otranto some years back, on the way to and from Corfu."

"Then you have the advantage of me, Mr Bennet, for I have never gone within a hundred leagues of the place. It would be my death, certainly politically and possibly literally, to leave the Curia for so long. But I understand you are a well-travelled gentleman, Mr Bennet."

All this time we had been progressing through various corridors, and now came out into a sunny courtyard, where a plain, unmarked coach awaited us. It was not until we had entered and settled into its cushioned seats that we were able to continue our conversation.

"I fear such prolonged absence from one's diocese would be frowned upon in England, your Grace," I ventured. "Or, should it be your Reverence? I have never addressed a Cardinal before."

"The correct form is 'your Eminence'. I see that, like most of your countrymen, you are an adherent of your heretical sect, Mr Bennet. Can I not persuade you to embrace the true faith?"

"At the risk of sounding like Pontius Pilate, your Eminence, what is the true faith? I find much to admire in the church of Rome, it is true, but also in my own church of England. I have friends who profess the orthodox faith, too, and it cannot be denied that their arguments are attractive."

"Ah! You would pick and choose! Then you are indeed a heretic. The most dangerous kind of heretic, and the most common, I fear."

"I confess to being guilty of αἴρεσις,[11] of choosing to believe what I consider most reasonable. I would not presume to bandy theology with a prince of the church, however. But did not your own Holy Father Leo the ninth choose to add to the creed a clause which had never been accepted by an ecumenical council, but only by a minor, provincial one, in Spain?"

He smiled, and bowed his head in acknowledgement.

"Lord Pennworth warned me you were a learned man, Mr Bennet, and I see he was not mistaken. But such talk is not healthy in Rome, where not only walls have ears. Let us speak of something else. What brings you to the eternal city?"

"I am here for the sake of my health, sir."

"Then let me, for the sake of your health, Mr Bennet, advise you to be more moderate, more restrained in your dealings and your opinions in public areas. My colleagues of the Holy Office are no doubt necessary, but they can, sometimes, be possessed of rather too much zeal for the faith."

---

[11] Hairesis : choice, in Greek.

"I thank you for the advice, your Eminence, but may I enquire whether you are in any way related to the Prince of Arsoli, and if so, is it true that you are a descendant of the great Cunctator?"

"As to that, sir, I can only repeat what my cousin said to Bonaparte when asked the same question. *'Je ne saurais en effet le prouver, c'est un bruit qui ne court que depuis douze cents ans dans notre famille.'*[12] But every family has its skeleton in the cupboard, I dare say."

This prompted me to complement him on his command of the English language, which led to the revelation that his mother had been English, and had always spoken to him in her mother tongue.

"She was Lady Cressida Flyte before she married my father," he explained, leaving me to make the connections with the Marchmain family.

In such small talk the rest of the journey to the *Albergo del Tonno was* rapidly consumed.

Reluctant as I was to prolong this interview, I could scarce refrain from inviting my rescuer to join us all so that we might express our gratitude for his assistance. To my great relief, he declined, and I was able to congratulate myself that I could at least speak freely of my experience with my family.

I could also congratulate myself that *Monsignor's* omniscience was not quite as comprehensive as he believed it to be, for he stopped the coach outside the Pantheon. I made sure to enter the inn, whence we had decamped

---

[12] I can't really prove it, but it's a rumour that's been going around for at least twelve hundred years.

weeks ago, making sure that any spies the Cardinal may have left saw me do so.

I believe they did not see me leave by the door into the Via del Seminario, nor my process from there to the slopes of the Pincian hill where I congratulate myself that we still remain undiscovered. So great and all-embracing is the network of police spies in Rome, that this can not be expected to remain safe for much longer.

My welcome was not precisely what I had looked for. The gentlemen, as might be expected, were discreet enough, with a 'good to see you back' from Bingley and an 'everything sorted?' from Morland, but the ladies were a different matter.

Jane merely hugged and kissed, saying "Thank God you are safe, Papa. You cannot know how worried we were." Your mother, however, from whom I might have been forgiven for expecting relief and gratitude was of quite a different mind.

"Mr Bennet! Mr Bennet!" she cried. "How can you be so cruel, so heartless as to get yourself arrested and leave your poor wife and daughter alone and helpless in a strange land? Whatever were we to do should you not come back? When they told me you had been taken away by the police, I quite swooned away. What I should have done had dear Mr Bingley not recollected your letter from Lord Pennworth (such an obliging gentleman, and so useful a connection, and you were going to waste it)... what I should have done without it I do not know. And why should you want to go grubbing about in holes in the ground at your age? I am sure you only do it to annoy me. If anything had happened to you and that odious Mr Collins had turned me out of Longbourn to starve on the streets, then how should you have liked it? You never think..."

There was much more on those lines, as you may imagine. In vain did I protest that I had not set out to invite arrest, that I was doing useful work in furthering knowledge of the ancient world, that I had not left her alone and friendless, that all had turned out well in the end etc.etc.

You know your mother, Lizzie, dear, and you may guess how long we should have stood in the hallway, discussing (for I will not say 'arguing') had not Margaret and Arianna appeared down the stairs, carrying between them a large, flat, rectangular object, covered with a sheet.

I recognised the sheet, with which I had once become intimately acquainted, and thought I recognised their burden, too, so it was no great surprise, and a welcome diversion when Margaret announced –

"It is done. Finished at last, or as near finished as may be, while we are here. It will need some touching up, and varnishing, and framing properly before it goes to the Academy, but I am at the stage where I long to be told I have done the right thing, so I thought we might have our own, private hanging day."

"What could be more appropriate?" I replied. "Hanging has been on my mind most of the day."

Along with burning, garrotting and various other delightful pastimes, but I felt it best to keep the rest to myself for the moment.

By the way, I have just noticed the date at the head of this screed. Please be assured, this is not a joke. It is so serious that I fear there will be no more letters for quite some time. I will keep a journal, however, of our adventures, and hope to be able to send it on to you before very long.

Until then, pray forgive your suddenly inordinately cautious and suspicious father,

F. Bennet

Chapter Thirty-eight : Mr Bennet's Journal – Hanging Day

Margaret had evidently given some thought to this event for she appeared to know just where to position the easel – which Arianna had produced from somewhere – so as to catch the light just so. Having done so, and placed her precious canvas on the pegs, she stood to one side and implored us to deal gently with her creation.

At another word, Arianna removed the sheet, with a flourish, and we all stood, gaping.

We have none of us ever really appreciated just how good a painter Margaret really is, I think. I remember her water colours in Corfu, of course, and the portraits she made for Lydia's friends there, and her sketches in Germany and Italy, but this was on a different level altogether.

We had seen the work of *Messieurs* David and Ingres in Paris, and this was like theirs, but without that feeling of grandiloquence and braggadocio that you so often get in modern French painting. The Classical subject matter was similar, the costumes were very similar, in Aspasia's case very much like Sappho's in David's image, but somehow the atmosphere was much more subtle, less declamatory.

I am talking nonsense, I know, but perhaps you will understand when you see it yourself. I will restrain myself to a brief description instead of more lyrical waxing now.

Pericles is seated on a terrace, looking out over his city, his chin resting on one hand, while his arm, in turn, rests on the balustrade. His well-known Corinthian helm is on the floor by his chair. No 'odeon for a crown' for him when he is at home. In the background is the city of Athens. I dare say it looks nothing like. Who knows, after all, what Athens looks like these days, let alone two thousand years ago? The shining mass of the Parthenon on top of the rocky Acropolis is unmistakeable, however.

At the opposite end of the canvas, Aspasia is entering through the door, and stopping to gaze at her lover. The look of joy and adoration on her face as she catches sight of him I am completely unable to describe, but I truly believe I have never seen it done better by anything in all the galleries of Europe.

I am biased, naturally, since both figures are instantly recognisable to those in the know. Or partly recognisable. There is no mystery about Pericles, although I am sure I am neither so handsome, nor so thin, nor so muscular nor so hirsute in real life, and I have never worn a beard.

The real surprise was Aspasia, however. In the painting, she is, in both pose and costume, so like the Venus de Milo that there must have been a connection in the mind of the painter.

But the surprise was not below Aspasia's hips, but above her neck for the face looking across the canvas was not Arianna, nor a mirror image of Margaret, nor even an unknown model, but Jane.

"Jane!" I gasped. "But you said..."

"I know what I said, but I had not seen Margaret's marvellous work then. I had not seen how perfectly she captured you, Papa. And Margaret can be very persuasive."

"But..." I continued to object, "but..."

"But what, Papa? The bare torso? I have always wondered at how so many ancient Grecians seemed to be able to keep their garments from falling below hip level while they never seem to stay on their shoulders. Pericles has the same problem, as you see. But fear not. The bare bosoms are not mine, they are Arianna's."

What could I say?

"It is a masterpiece, my dear, my dears, that is, all my dears. I long to see it on the wall at the Academy. But I hope the paint is properly dry, for it must be packed away now. Everything must be packed away, for we are no longer safe in Rome.

We must flee."

Chapter Thirty-nine : Mrs Morland to Mrs Darcy – Flight

Capua

May Day 1837

Dear Elizabeth,

Your father is not feeling quite the thing just now, and has asked me to write to assure you that all is well. Jane and Mrs Bennet are taking turns nursing him, while James bemoans the impossibility of treating him without access to a decent apothecary. I do not think it is anything to worry about, and neither does James, which is perhaps more important, but under the circumstances it is rather inconvenient.

You will be wondering just what those 'circumstances' are, I dare say. I saw the last letter Mr Bennet wrote to you, before he sent it to be secretly transmitted, and I can only guess at the suspense and consternation in which it must have left you.

It certainly left *us* in a great deal of consternation when Mr Bennet made his shocking announcement. After all, no-one expects the Spanish Inquisition. The Austrian spy watching us in Venice a few years ago had been rather a joke, he was so obvious. Not so in Rome. We had noticed no-one following us about except the usual beggars and mountebanks.

I could not believe my old friend was in earnest at first.

"Fie on you, Mr Bennet," I cried, "to upset your own daughter so, to say nothing of the rest of us, for a mere laugh. This joke is no more worthy of your true wit than it is funny!"

"It is no joke, my dear," he replied, and recounted his morning's adventures.

There was little we could say to any of it. It was undeniably true that he had been taken away by the police. I had witnessed that myself. It was also undeniable that my own James had gone with Charles Bingley to petition Lord Pennworth's cardinal friend on Mr Bennet's behalf.

"We must take advantage of the Cardinal's information being out of date while we can," Mr Bennet insisted, "and leave while we still can."

Your sister Jane was far from convinced, however.

"There must be some mistake," she said. "Surely such things are the stuff of history and of sensationalism nowadays! The Spanish Inquisition, indeed! In this day and age! And, in any case, did not Cardinal Whotsisname say that he could protect us?"

"Yes, he did. For a price. And who knows what that price might be, or when he might present us with his bill. I do not choose to continue in Rome under such terms. Do you?"

"But, the Spanish Inquisition? Surely that died out long ago?"

"I think I have good reason to believe that the Spanish Inquisition is alive and well and living in Rome as we speak. And if that is not the case, why should the Cardinal attempt to deceive me?"

"True. I cannot believe that a clergyman – even a Popish clergyman – would tell a lie about such a thing. Yet I cannot believe that there are still fanatics who, in the name of religion, will sweep innocent people off the streets and subject them to torments and death."

"This will not do," said Mr Bennet. "You never will be able to make both the Inquisitor and the Cardinal good for anything. Take your choice, but you must be satisfied with only one. There is but such a quantity of truth between them; just enough to make one good sort of man; and of late it has been shifting about pretty much. For my part, I am inclined to believe it all the Cardinal's, but you shall do as you choose."

Objections continued to be voiced, especially as no-one else had noticed anything untoward while we were staying near the Pantheon. We had just got comfortably ensconced in our new lodgings, and were all the more loath to remove all over again, still less to flee the country.

Mr Bennet was adamant, however.

"I understand why you do not want to move," he said. "I do not want to move myself. I have just started on a new and very promising line of research, and the last thing I want is to be forced to abandon it. You may think I am making too much of this incident. You may be right. But you were not there. You cannot know what it felt like. You cannot know what it feels like now, to know that at any time I may be taken up and incarcerated − or worse; who knows what would have happened had the Cardinal not turned up when he did? Still worse, it might happen to any of us. How would you feel, Bingley, if Jane were to be carried off thus? Or you, Morland, if it were to happen to Margaret? I know how I should feel if Mrs Bennet were to fall into such hands. Which reminds me, where is Mrs Bennet?"

Embarrassed looks all round. Shuffling of feet, too.

Bingley spoke up first.

"Mrs Bennet is out with her..."

"Mama is gone to a party with Count Posca," interrupted Jane. "She said she would be late back."

"And she is gone alone? With no-one to... to accompany her?"

"She has been accustomed to do that for some time now, Papa. Did you not know? We all thought it must be with your blessing, or, at least, consent."

"And no-one thought to tell me? Does anyone even know where she is gone? Well, I am served aright for my complacency. Let us all go to bed, then, and enjoy the sleep of the just, for there is nothing more we may do until the wanderer returns."

Alas, the courier is growing urgent for his packet, and I must leave you in suspense and the hope that this arcane method of communication forced upon us by circumstances will somehow enable you to read this one day.

The explanation of the arcane circumstances must wait for another opportunity, I fear, but until then, rest assured that we are all well, mosquito bites excepted, and that you are never far from the thoughts of

Your fugitive friend,

Margaret Morland.

Chapter Forty: Mr Bennet to Mrs Darcy - Unexpected Decisions

Naples
15 May 1837

My dear Lizzie,

Pray excuse the time which I have so idly let pass since my last letter. Pray also excuse the spindly handwriting. The two are not entirely unconnected.

I recollect I told you in my last letter that I believed that our party were under observation by the authorities here in Rome, and that we did not care to continue under such conditions. Our removal to our new lodgings appeared to have thrown our watchers off the scent for the time being, but there was no telling how long that would remain the case.

My own inclination was to leave instantly, but in real life that is much easier said than done. For one thing, while I held my council of war on my return from my stint with the Inquisition, Mrs Bennet was still adorning some dance floor with her Roman Count. For another, we had a great deal to pack and organise, and very little in the way of transport. For yet another, we had bills to pay, if we did not want to be followed by debt-collectors as well as by government agents.

We did not want to be followed by anyone at all, but that, it appears, is as little to be obtained in Rome as in Venice.

A new council had to be held over breakfast, where everything must be told over again for your mother's benefit.

"Mister Bennet!" was her reaction, "What things you say! We cannot just go home, just like that."

"No, indeed," I replied. "We cannot, for home is too far away, and not to be reached on foot, but we must arrange transport to somewhere, and that with as little noise as may be, for I fear that, if our imminent departure comes to the ears of certain persons in authority in this city, we may be prevented."

"But why should that be? Whatever makes you say that?"

"You would know the answer to both those questions had you been here yesterday, or even last night, instead of out with your... Instead of elsewhere. Where were you, by the way?"

Fortunately, at this point, the others stepped in, or else words might have been said which were best unspoken. I make it a point never to believe rumours, but I was beginning to wonder.

"Papa was taken up yesterday," said Jane, "by the police, and interrogated by the Inquisition."

"Don't be silly, Jane, darling," your mother replied, "Everyone knows the Spanish Inquisition only exists in sensational novels. Besides, we are in Italy."

"Yet he was questioned by them yesterday. Ask him yourself."

So she did, with the result that you may imagine.

Fortunately, I have long been accustomed to being told by Mrs Bennet not to be so silly, and her disbelief did not surprise me in any way. Nor did it affect the decision we had already made in her absence, not even when she objected that she could not possibly leave without saying goodbye to Count Posca.

What did affect it was the return of James Morland from his morning stroll, which, it turned out, had taken him to the nearest city gate, Rome still being encircled by its ancient walls, whose gates serve as convenient places for checking the comings and goings of both residents and visitors.

The news he brought was not at all welcome.

"There are guards on all the gates, and they are checking the papers of everyone who comes and goes. We may kiss goodbye our chances of slipping away unnoticed."

You may guess how unwelcome to all of us such a revelation was. We were all at a stand for a moment.

Then your sister piped up.

"This is downright silly," she said. "Why should we not after all just go home, as normal people would? We are respectable people. We are English. We are not criminals, or agitators, or revolutionaries. Papa has had a brush with the police which has shaken him, but is there any other reason why we should up sticks and away? Is there any real reason for a clandestine departure? We have broken no law, after all."

"We do not need to have broken any law," I replied. "We are not in England now; there is no

Habeas Corpus, no presumption of innocence here. The police may take us all into custody any time they wish, and keep us there until we can prove to their satisfaction that we are innocent of any charge. The Cardinal made very sure to explain all this to me yesterday. We are English, and Protestant. Those two facts alone are enough to arouse suspicion. The government's spies have seen me meeting Signor Beppone, they have seen me entering the house of his friend, Beppino, both of whom are, apparently known agitators. They may have seen me, they may have seen Margaret in the tunnels, where revolutionaries and other unsavoury characters are known to meet. I have had bands of those sorts pointed out to me and been warned not to enter certain parts of the underworld there.

The Cardinal has promised us protection, but only, I think, if I act as his spy, and I have no intention of doing that.

At the moment we have an opportunity. By moving from the inn, we have avoided our surveillance, we are immune from observation by the authorities. That immunity will not last for long. We shall be found eventually. We may wake up tomorrow morning and find a spy outside, taking his ease in the square. After that, we will live every moment in fear of being taken up and incarcerated. For myself, I might take the risk, but for my friends, and particularly for the ladies, I would certainly not. Pray forgive my prolixity, my dears. I had not known myself to be so eloquent, but '*il fatto è serio*,' to quote from our hosts' own tongue."

"Oh, Mr Bennet, Mr Bennet," cried your mother, "do not let them clap you in gaol. Whatever should I do without you?"

I will spare you the discussion which followed, Lizzie, my love, but we eventually resolved to depart that evening, although I am inclined to think that resolution to have been taken, at least in part, to humour me."

I took very little part in this discussion, for its conclusion was inevitable, and I was pondering on practicalities, so that I only emerged from my study when I heard someone say –

"But how are we to leave, if all the gates are guarded, and the guards are ordered not to let us pass?"

"First we must find out whether they are truly barred against us," I said. "Unfortunately, I can think of no other way to do so than by trying to leave through them. We may as well pack our traps and make the attempt. If we are allowed to pass, then we may continue to Naples, where we will be well received, I am sure, by the friends we made there on our last Italian journey. If we are stopped, then we must take other counsel."

"But, if the authorities are truly looking for us," objected Bingley, "will the guards not take us all up and throw us into the Tullianum, or whatever they use these days, until the powers that be are satisfied?"

This found us at a stand. We could not take such a risk. And yet...

Fortunately, your old father is not yet completely senile, and still occasionally capable of rational thought.

"I have an idea," I said. "I do not know whether it is practical or not, but I do know how to find out. Let me make the attempt, but be ready to leave at any time. I must go out now, but I shall not be long, I hope."

"I think I know what you have in mind, Mr Bennet," Margaret intervened, "I think it involves someone whose name begins with B. Before resorting to such measures, do you not think it worth asking one of Mrs Bennet's noble Roman friends for help. Could not Count Posca, for instance do something?"

"Oh!" said your mother, "Oh! Antonio? He's gone away. Left me on my own (Io, cry I, but silently); he would not stay."

Universal cries of sympathy, coupled with questions on the line of 'why was that?', 'But I thought…' and so on.

"So," I said, (well, I had to say something) "do you wish to tell us about it, my dear?"

"Oh, Mr Bennet, Mr Bennet, I have been sadly deceived! I have nourished a serpent in my bosom!"

"Not literally, I hope, my dear?"

"Oh, Mr Bennet, how can you say such things? I mean his pretence of partiality to me was very agreeable. You cannot know how agreeable it can be for a lady who is not so very young any more to have a handsome young gentleman – no, a handsome young nobleman – in attendance upon her. Especially when her husband neglects her for another – for piles of old stones. But it was all a pretence. Last night at the ball he came out with it. He has been in the habit of asking me for small sums to pay his bills, and I have advanced him I cannot tell how much over the past weeks, apart from the presents I have bought him, and my contributions to his aunt's charities. But last night he said he must have five thousand scudi, on the spot, in coin or as a banker's draft, or he would be forced to leave Rome to avoid his creditors. I was shocked, as you may well believe, Mr Bennet. I have no real idea how much five thousand scudi might be in real money. I cannot keep up with all these foreign coins, and leave all that to you, my dear. But however much a scudi is worth, five thousand of them must be a lot of money.

He was very vague about the creditors he must pay off, but most insistent they must be paid, instantly. I gave him what was in my purse, and told him I did not carry such sums about with me.

He would have had us come directly back to here, where there must be some draft on an English bank to be cashed. He even suggested I sign a note of hand, or what I took to be a note of hand, for it was all in Italian, for the sum. It was then that the scales fell from my eyes, for he must have had such a document prepared in advance, and had come to meet me purely in search of money.

I refused, of course, and told him to come tomorrow and we would discuss it with you, Mr Bennet. He turned round and walked away, without another word, and the next time I saw him he was dancing with a young lady who I knew to be the unmarried daughter of a prominent banker.

He did not return, although I waited to the end of the party. I had little choice in the matter, for I was penniless and had neither transport nor escort to bring me back here.

If it had not been for Princess Aldobrandini taking pity on me and offering me a lift in her carriage, I do not know what I should have done. Do not scold me, I beg, for I am already wretched at having been deceived so."

Well, you may imagine, Lizzy, that there was much I could have said, but it would not have served in the moment, so I merely said,

"Well, you are back now, and safe and sound, and we are going home. I am glad to have you back, my dear, and we shall laugh at all this when we get back to Longbourn. I must go now to make arrangements for just that, but I will be back soon."

"But what of all my new dresses that are in the making? What of the hats and the baubles and the mosaics? Who will collect them and pay for them?"

This was a dilemma, for I must be about my necessary business.

Bingley turned up trumps, however.

"Give me a list of all the bills outstanding, and I will go the rounds and pay them all. We may settle up at our leisure."

While this excellent design was being debated, I took the opportunity, after thanking Bingley, to set off on my errand.

But my attention has just been drawn to the undeniable fact that this letter is growing to resemble something more like a novel, and the steamer is waiting, so I will close now and spend the time on the next leg of our voyage in composing a narrative of how we escaped from Rome, and what we encountered after we had done so.

I can promise you no tales of derring-do or any great adventures, but the enterprise was not without its incidents.

What I can promise you is that we all survived and retained our health and our liberty, and hope to be with you shortly.

Until then, I must beg you to indulge

Your regrettably verbose and annoyingly mysterious father,

F. Bennet

Chapter Forty-one : Mr Bennet to Mrs Darcy – A Walk in the Dark

Naples

18 May 1837

Dear Lizzie,

I owe you an apology for keeping you waiting for this relation of our adventures on the way home, occasioned entirely by my own inability to be laconic. I promise to be less prolix this time.

Cast your mind back, my dear, to our last day at the house on the Pincio.

By now I was sufficiently well known to the Beppos as to be confident of finding one at any time of the day.

I was in luck, and fell in with Beppone at the first low dive I tried.

When I told him what I had in mind he said such a thing could not be done. What I wanted did not exist, or it was too dangerous, or too expensive, or a thousand other reasons which he did not propose to explain. It is remarkable, however, what the sight of a few good English guineas will do in these situations, and eventually he agreed to introduce me to someone who might be able to help us.

That someone, to my surprise, turned out to be sitting at the table by the door, and, even more surprisingly, did not go by the name of Beppo.

"*Mi chiamono il Lupone*," he replied to my enquiry how to address him, accompanying the sobriquet with the appropriate snarl. *"Non parlo Inglese."*

The negotiations that followed would have been quite enough to bring on a headache in English. In a mixture of Italian and dumb show, you may imagine how trying they were.

Fortunately, I had Beppone to help. I placed no great reliance on his impartiality; he was far from disinterested in the proceedings, but as a last resort translator he had his uses. I am aware of the Italian proverb, *'il traduttore è il tradittore'*[13], but I could detect no obvious collusion, and remained satisfied that my wants were adequately conveyed : secret departure from the city, with transport thereafter to Naples, the whole for three ladies and three gentlemen and their baggage.

"Una valigia per persona, non di piu," was the only stipulation made by Signor Lupone. Then we really got down to basics.

"Seicento scudi. Adesso." Was the starting demand.

This was obviously ridiculous. At five scudi to the guinea (forgive, me, dear Lizzy, I cannot quite believe in these new-fangled sovereigns, and still think in guineas), that would be L120.

"Treicento," I countered.

A smile worthy of his animal namesake lit up the smuggler's face, and we proceeded to the real negotiation. The ins and outs of this process were tortuous enough, to be sure, with a great deal of histrionics on both sides. I had not thought

---

[13] The translator is the traitor.

myself so devoted to Thespis before, but I blessed him by the end of the performance.

We settled in the end on four hundred and fifty, or, rather, we settled for ninety guineas, the sight of English gold working its usual magic. There could be no question of payment in advance. I did not come down with the last shower of rain. I gave him the twenty guineas I had on me, and promised to pay the rest on arrival at our destination.

There remained only a rendezvous to set.

"Ai vespri, nei grotti, alla stanza delle scimmie,[14]*"* growled Mr Wolf.

"Capito," I replied. *"Allora, ai vespri."*

I knew the room he meant, and so did Beppone. Now there only remained the task of persuading the others, and especially the ladies, to trust themselves to a self-confessed villain.

As it turned out, the ladies were more reluctant to trust themselves to a ladder into a dark hole than to a smuggler.

"Let us be honest," remarked your sister Jane, after I had warned them of the perils of the route I proposed.

"We will be relying on a smuggler for guidance. But have not all of us relied on smugglers at some time, if only for brandy and coffee? Have we ever found one untrustworthy?"

"Those were at least English criminals, however," observed her husband. "Can we place the same reliance on Italians?"

---

[14] At vespers, in the caves, at the room of the apes.

"All the same," I warned. "If anyone is afraid of the big, bad wolf, now is the time to say so,"

"I do not think we are afraid of him," replied Jane. "But I am far from happy about entrusting myself to this ladder you talk of."

"Well, I am not afraid," added Margaret, "of the ladder, nor of the smuggler and all his gang. Are we not English? And do not we not have our menfolk to protect us? I have one question, however."

"What is that?" I asked.

"Only this," she replied, with a suspiciously sweet smile on her face. "Will we at least be permitted to ask Mr Wolf what time it is?"

It was not as easy as that, naturally. The one bag rule, particularly, caused lots of trouble, and not only with the ladies. I admit to being guilty in that respect myself, in trying to take all my exhibits home with me, and the Doctor had a whole grisly trunkful of pickled specimens provided by his Italian colleagues. Each one of us, I believe, had something that could not be parted with.

Reason prevailed in the end, however, and it was Morland who delivered the compelling argument.

"We have yet three months on the lease of this place," he pointed out. "If we take too much with us now, it is all but certain we shall lose something. Why should we not stow everything away behind locked doors and take the key away with us? When we reach a friendlier haven we could then find someone who is in good odour with the authorities here to come and collect our traps for us. There is a risk, I agree, but no greater than entrusting things to a carrier. I am sure Prince Filippo will be able to recommend an honest tradesman who will do the job."

So, limiting ourselves to essentials (and a very few other items) that is what we did.

There was a delay at the last minute, when Bingley remarked,

"But you have miscounted, Mr Bennet. Three couples is what you told your nefarious friend, if I understand correctly. You have completely forgotten about poor Arianna. Surely, we cannot abandon her thus?"

"I have not forgotten about Arianna," I replied, "except to mention her just now. I have a particular task for her, one that will make your bill-paying errand unnecessary, and at the same time cause our departure to be less remarked. The idea came to me while I was negotiating our passage. I intend to leave her here in charge of all the bits and pieces we cannot take with us. She will give out that we are all down with the marsh fever and in no case to see anyone or go out. She will pay bills as they come in. I will leave her a store of money for this, and for her own keep, for the duration of the lease."

"But this is but abandonment by another name."

"Not so, for before the lease is out, we shall have reached a place of safety, in Naples, say, or Genoa, whence we may despatch a trusted carrier to bring all our effects to us, with Arianna to oversee the passage. It is a great charge to lay upon a servant, I know, but I am confident that she will not let us down. But thank you for reminding me, Bingley, for I must speak to Arianna now."

Arianna, when spoken to, entered into the plan with gusto.

"*Μην ανησυχείς κύριε Μπεννετε,*" she said, "*Θα κρατήσω ϲα πάνϲα ασφαλή μέχρι να με σϲείλεις.*"

Arianna does this lapsing into her native tongue when she wishes to be particularly serious. It particularly distresses Mrs Bennet, who steadfastly refuses to learn a word of any foreign language. Fortunately, my comprehension of Demotic Greek is much better than my attempts at reproducing the barbarous noises to which the current inhabitants of the land of Plato and Aristotle have reduced the beautiful tongue of the ancients, and I took comfort from her assurance that she would keep everything safe until I sent for her.

Now I had but to convince your mother that she could manage a journey to Naples without a lady's maid to keep her presentable. Still that was nothing compared to the struggle I anticipated when she eventually saw the route we would be taking.

I shall continue this in the morning, for here comes Morland with his bitter draughts, the reason for which I have not yet explained. Till then, pray, bear with

Your excessively prolix father,

F. Bennet.

Chapter Forty-two : Mr Bennet to Mrs Darcy - Moles and Marsh Fever

Naples
21 May 1837

Dear Lizzie,

Forgive the disjointed narration, but we are all feeling a trifle disjointed just now. The reason for this I hope to make clear before I finish this letter at last.

I left you having received Arianna's assurance that she would keep our belongings safe while we escaped from the undue attention of the Roman authorities. I will try to be more brief on this sheet, and to that end I will spare you the rest of our preparations, and the disagreements and subterfuges that accompanied them.

Suffice it to say that as the bells rang out for Vespers we were perched in Beppino's yard, waiting for our turn on the ladder. Margaret went first, by right of having done this before, and I stayed till last, confident that all my powers of persuasion and assistance would very soon be needed.

I admit that staring at a hole in the ground with the top of a long, narrow ladder sticking out of it is not the most encouraging way to begin a journey, but all went well, in spite of dubious looks and comments on the line's of 'are you sure all this is necessary, Mr Bennet?'. All went well, that is, until it came to be your mother's turn.

"Oh, Mr Bennet, Mr Bennet!" she cried out as I was offering her my arm, "I cannot possibly climb down into that black hole! Surely such lengths are not necessary?"

In vain did I point out that all the rest of our party, including her own daughter, were already down the black hole, that I myself had been down it many times, as had her good friend Margaret, and that there were, to my certain knowledge, no spiders, worms nor other creepy crawlies down there, to say nothing of assorted bogeymen.

"But I cannot possibly climb down that awful ladder," she persisted. "It bends, and it wobbles! I shall fall, I know I shall fall, and then what will you do, Mr Bennet?"

"Why, I shall catch you, or, at least, pick you up again, my love, for it is no great distance to fall, and the ground is soft at the bottom. But perhaps we may not need to go to such lengths, for here is Beppino with a length of nice, stout rope, which I shall tie about your waist, thus, and we shall both of us lower you gently to the ground should you miss your footing on the ladder."

The look with which she greeted this announcement was so far beyond dubious as to exceed my powers of description, but as I had suited my actions to my words, and was now actually in the process of guiding her feet onto the treads of the ladder, she fell silent, and reluctantly began climbing down.

I do not think I was ever more proud of your mother, Lizzie, than when I saw her go down that hole. Of course, it was quite a while before the cries of 'Oh! Mr Bennet!' died away, even after she had reached the bottom of the shaft, but I followed her as soon as I could, and we all gathered round to comfort her, while Beppino followed me and the ladder was withdrawn before the flagstone was replaced.

The pitch darkness that ensued did nothing to improve Mrs Bennet's nerves, and they were my constant companion through the days that followed, but, fortunately, Beppino had come prepared and we had to wait but a moment before he struck his flint and put a light to the first of the four lanterns lying waiting there for us. The other three were soon lit and distributed among the ladies, whose murmurs diminished when they could see where they were.

Our guide led us along corridors which were familiar to two of our group. In truth, I think I could have found the way myself, but with the ladies present we must be sure of our way. As we came to the first of the wall paintings, the female murmurings began to grow again but in tones more of wonder than of fear.

"Where are we, Papa?" asked Jane. "Is this where you have been disappearing to every day for weeks now? What is this place?"

"The answer to your second question is yes, my dear," I replied. "The answer to the others is rather more difficult. Everyone I have asked about this place – and I have been careful of whom I enquired, as you may imagine – has merely called it '*Le grotte sepolte*', which, as you know, is simply 'The buried grottos' in Italian. I have a theory, however. I think we are in the remains of the famous '*Domus Aurea*', the Golden Palace of the emperor Nero."

"What? The wicked emperor who burnt all the Christians, and the city of Rome with them?"

"Just so, my dear, and this is not a mere supposition, either. I have my reasons for believing so. Its size and position, and the quality of its decorations, even in this state, all fit the literary descriptions."

"But, surely, the emperor's palace could not have been subterranean? Who would build such a place?"

"It was not built underground. We have long known that the Flavian Amphitheatre, the building we now call the Colosseum, was built on the site of the southern portion of the *Domus Aurea*. I believe that Vespasian wished to leave no memento of his predecessor visible, and had the rest of the building buried at the same time, possibly using the rubble and spoil from the building of his amphitheatre. That, and nearly two thousand years of accretions, have resulted in the hill we see today."

"It seems hardly possible, Papa, but I would never doubt you. Yet, to build an entire hill is such an undertaking!"

"And yet, we have visible proof that the ancient Romans were capable of such things. We have all marvelled at the *Bocca della Verità*, have we not? Do you remember the steep hill facing that church?

The Romans of today call it *Monte Testaccio*, Potsherd Mountain, and that is what it is. It is the rubbish heap of the ancient city, largely consisting of cast-off, broken pots and suchlike, under a layer of the dust of two millennia and more. I shall write a paper on the subject when we get home, but I must restrain myself at the moment, for we are come to the place of our rendezvous."

At the end of the corridor, a light could be seen in the octagonal chamber. Soon we should know our fate. Either our new guide awaited us there, or he had betrayed us, and we should find the forces of the Inquisition, or the Roman police, awaiting us.

I am sorry, Lizzie my dear, I could not help trying to inject a little suspense into my narration, however pointless such efforts must be, for if it were the Inquisition, I should not be writing this.

Mister Wolf had not let us down, however, and his emissary stood waiting for us with a much bigger lantern in his hand. On seeing us, he nodded to Beppino, who bowed to us and departed, leaving us to fend for ourselves with my new acquaintance.

The latter said nothing, but motioned us to follow him, leaving me to shepherd my flock into the corridor he took, the one that Beppino had specifically warned me against as being the haunt of *maledetti*.

"*Alea iacta est*," I could not resist saying as we filed into the darkness. The advantages of a classical education are such a comfort, are they not?

I will not dwell on how long we spent winding along our subterranean path, or what treasures we glimpsed on the way. I was at the rear of the column, while our guide led the way, and very soon lost all sense of direction and of time. It seemed aeons had passed before the noise of something being dragged across the floor, and a glimpse of daylight up ahead presaged an end to our pioneering.

We came out into a square chamber, dimly lit from an open doorway directly ahead of us. The stone walls still bore traces of plaster and paint, the latter so faint as to be scarcely made out.

We did not linger, but emerged, blinking, into the daylight, where I was relieved to make out the lean features of Mr Wolf himself.

"Oh, Mr Bennet, Mr Bennet," your mother cried, "wherever can we be?"

I looked around me, and instantly knew the answer.

"We are outside the walls of Rome," I replied. "We are on the Appian Way, outside one of the tombs that line the roadway. That tower in the distance is, if I am not mistaken the tomb of Caecilia Metella, which your favourite poet apostrophised."

Blank looks all round.

"We were here some weeks ago, or, rather, at the Metella tomb. You remember the *Capi di Bove*, the ox heads about the top of the tower? I think it was Margaret who quoted Lord Byron.

> *'What was this tower of strength? Within its cave What treasure lay so lock'd, so hid?—A woman's grave."*

"Do you not remember?"

"Then we are away? We may take our ease now?"

"Not quite. We are still on Papal territory. We must continue until we reach Neapolitan soil. This is the Appian Way. It is a hundred and forty four *milia passuum* to Capua, which is the first place of any size where we may feel safe. That is some hundred and thirty miles in English, and I trust our Italian friends have made arrangements for our conveyance, for otherwise we shall have a very long walk."

As if we had been overheard, Signor Lupone gave a shrill whistle, and the rest of his band emerged from the trees that lined the road. With them they brought three carts, one empty, another apparently loaded with straw, and a third piled high with all sorts of bundles and boxes. The last to emerge from the bushes was a boy, leading a string of mules.

This, evidently, was our transport. I had had no great hopes of a carriage, but this was a disappointment to say the least.

For the first time since the grottos, Lupone opened his mouth.

"Le donne si siederanno sulla paglia," he said. *"I signori devono cavalcare I muli."*[15]

While the ladies settled themselves as comfortably as might be on the straw, the rest of us took a good look at our mounts.

"Has anyone ever ridden a mule?" I asked.

"Not I," replied Bingley, while Morland merely shook his head, while eying his beast with a doubtful gaze.

"Well, I dare say we shall soon get the knack, although the beasts have a wicked reputation. We shall have the best part of a week to find out."

Before we could mount, however, we had another ceremony to perform. Mr Wolf had

---

[15] The ladies may sit on the straw. The gentlemen will have to ride the mules.

entered into the secrecy of our departure with what I believe to be malicious glee.

Our good, English hats were taken from us and replaced by great, battered wheels of straw, while over all we must wear black cloaks, ragged but voluminous, which covered us from head to foot. The ladies were not spared this costume, and must also remove their shoes and socks, which were stowed out of sight beneath the straw.

"I say," Bingley remarked at this point, "I don't know that I like all this."

"Nor I," countered Morland, "but I can see the point of it. Got up like this, we look for all the world like a band of travelling tinkers, at whom no troop of carabinieri would look twice. They are looking for English gentlefolk, not Italian ruffians. To be authentic we really should be scruffier, and the ladies should have dirty feet."

He was right, of course, and the disguise served us well several times that first day, when we were overtaken by groups of armed police who galloped past without a second glance. But, oh the torment of jolting along on those hard saddles, all muffled up in a thick, stinking cape whose black colour soaked up every ounce of heat from the relentless sun of an Italian spring!

By the end of the day we were drooping in our saddles, and were still barely ten miles from the city. I, for one, was dreaming of a comfortable bed and a wholesome meal, but it was not to be. As the sun set we turned off the road into a grove of trees where, in a wide, but hidden clearing, a brooklet chattered down the slope.

Our guides instantly set to, erecting two large tents in some sort of felten material, while collecting sticks and making a fire. They had obviously done this before, for it took only a few minutes before one of them was stirring something in a copper cauldron above a roaring fire.

Another produced a large jar of wine, and Mr Wolf motioned to us to sit by the fire and eat with them.

The meat was unfamiliar and best left nameless, as was the yellow mush with which it was served, but both were grateful to an empty stomach. The wine was quite as rough as might be imagined, and deceptively strong, and under its influence the language barrier began to break down. It helped that we had all picked up some Italian during the course of our travels, even if it was only Mrs Bennet's 'si' and 'no' and 'quanta costa?' with a few numbers and adjectives.

Our leader also proved to be not quite as devoid of English as he claimed to be, although his accent was at times difficult to follow. It turned out that, as a young boy, some thirty years previously, he had been party to the smuggling out of Rome of another English couple, 'Milord and Milady Eppurt'.

"*Il gran Visconte Eppurt e la sua bella moglie*," he said, as the wine loosened his tongue. "*Quello Inglese fu un eroe della guerra contro i francesi, di grande aiuto ai partigiani.*[16] You are English Milord, Signor Bennet, you know Visconte Eppurt ? 'E give my father this ring."

He removed a silver ring from his left hand, and held it up in the firelight, for all to see. It was a

---

[16] That Englishman was a hero in the war against the French, of great help to the partisans.

signet ring, with a crest engraved on it that meant nothing to me.

I was about to say that there were many English Milords, when I was interrupted.

"Wait!" said Margaret. "I know that crest. I have seen it many times. So have you, James, when visiting your sister Catherine."

"That is not the Tilney crest," replied Morland.

"No, but we have seen it at Northanger, and I remember where, now. On the coach door, when Henry's sister came to visit."

"Of course!" I cried. "Not 'Eppurt', but Ha'porth, spelt Hapworth. We are all familiar with Eleanor's tale of how they fled from Rome with Bonaparte's soldiers on their heels."

Lupone had obviously been following some of what was said.

"*Conosci Milord Visconte Eppurt?*" he asked.

"*Lo conosco,*" I replied. "*Noi lo conosciamo tutti. È il Conte di Pennworth ora, e per di più la signora Morland laggiù è sua sorella.*"[17]

My Italian is nowhere near good enough to cope with in-laws. Margaret's is better; let her explain the difference if she felt up to it. This announcement, however, caused a minor riot among our guides, and we all had to endure the embraces of excited Italians for quite some time, or so it seemed at least.

Margaret was the only one spared. Our friends contented themselves with fervid gazes, kneeling

---

[17] I know him. We all know him. He is the Earl of Pennworth now, and what is more, that lady over there is his sister.

and crossing themselves as if she were a goddess, or at least a saint.

Now the wine really began to flow, and my recollection becomes hazy, until waking up the following morning. It took some little time before I realised where I was, and that was not until after I had grasped the unaccustomed fact that I was lying on the ground, fully clothed and wrapped in my filthy black cloak from yesterday.

Our guides were seated around the fire, spooning some sort of porridge into their mouths with a ridiculously loud slurping noise, punctuated by howls and bellows fit to wake the dead. When they saw me move their cries became even more distressingly vociferous, almost drowning out the throbbing in my head.

One of them held out a bowl to me, and I tottered across to him and took it. It was the sun rising above the trees that did for me. I am sure it had not been nearly so bright the previous day, but now it struck my eyes with such a fiendishly bright beam that I must lay down my bowl and creep behind a bush where I instantly deposited the contents of my stomach, to the delighted howls of laughter of my companions.

This latest caterwauling brought Bingley and Morland from where they, too, lay prone by the fireside.

"Oh!" cried Bingley, "I think I am going to die."

"Lucky you," responded Morland. "I fear I am going to live."

At this point the ladies emerged from their tent, looking impossibly neat and collected.

"I trust you slept well, Mr Bennet?" your mother remarked. "But, oh! Mr Bennet, what are those red spots all over your face? And your hands too? Doctor, Doctor, can it be the dread smallpox or some other plague?"

"I think not, Mrs Bennet," Morland replied. "They look to me like insect bites of some sort. I have some, as well, and Mr Bingley likewise. It comes of leaving parts of our bodies exposed to the ministrations of the mosquitoes and suchlike during the night. You will have been spared, or relatively spared that in your tent.

It came back to me now. At the end of the regrettable carousing into which the evening had somehow lapsed, we had discovered that our smuggler friends intended to annex the larger tent for their own during the night, while the rest of us, ladies and gentlemen too, were expected to share the other.

For my part, if I had known what our chivalrous gesture in conceding the tent to the ladies was about to incur, I should have let propriety go hang. I believe Bingley and Morland would have agreed with me, but by the end of that day I was in no state to argue.

Somehow, we made our toilettes and broke our fast, and set off again on our way. The sun climbed higher in the sky, and shade was a rare commodity, the cultivated fields, crisscrossed with drainage or irrigation ditches, coming right up to the roadside.

It is not uncommon for a spring day in Italy to outdo for heat a summer's day in England, but that particular day was also particularly hot. Or so I felt, as I became increasingly incoherent in my thoughts and afflicted with shivering fits alternating with hot flushes.

When we stopped at last to make camp for the night, I fell, rather than dismounted from my mule. So they tell me, at any rate, for I have no recollection of such a thing.

I have no recollection of much, really, of the rest of our journey. There remain only disjointed vignettes – of lying in a sort of net, suspended from my mule's saddle, swaying and bumping along; of Morland dosing me with a bitter tea from time to time, and, at last, of crossing a bridge, and hearing Lupone say –

"Ecco il Fiume Garigliano. Siamo nelle Due Sicilie. Ora siete al securo, signori, signore."[18]

---

[18] Behold the River Garigliano. We are in the Two Sicilies. You are in safety, ladies and gentlemen.

Chapter Forty-three : Mr Bennet to Mrs Darcy - Bella Napoli

Naples
25 May 1837

That was the last night we spent on the road, and the following morning I was myself again, if a little weak and shaken.

Morland pronounced me well on the way to recovery.

"You had a fever," he said. "Quite a serious one. Our guides were adamant in calling it Marsh Fever, contracted from the miasma arising from the ground near the spring that, night we spent in the open. Personally, I think all those insect bites might have had something to do with it, but I acknowledge my colleagues do not think much of my idea. Whatever the source, there was no doubt of the outcome, however, and I flatter myself I know how to treat an ague when I see one. I was half expecting something of the sort, and laid in a good stock of Peruvian Bark, which was just as well, for most of it is gone now. You will do, now, I think, but you must not over-exert yourself. It may come back yet. These things often do."

God bless you, Morland, is what I say. Bless me, how many times have I needed to say that? I am sure the Jesuit's Bark saved me, but what really set me up was sleeping in a bed again when we got to Capua at last.

Here we parted with our guides, making sure to reward them well, even though they protested at being paid to help the family of the English hero.

From there it was but a short stage, in a real coach, even if it was only a diligence, to Caserta, whence another day's journey brought us to Bella Napoli.

Our old friend Prince Catapani welcomed us to his palazzo as if he had been waiting for us all along, which cannot possibly have been the case.

The welcome began almost as soon as the street door of the Palazzo Catapani was opened to our knocks.

The scowling face of the old retainer who grudgingly opened it a crack was unknown to Jane and Bingley, but very familiar to the rest of us.

"*Salve, Sigismondo*," piped up Mrs Morland, while I was still arranging my tenses in my head. "*I vagabondi sono tornati, come tu vedi. Com è sua Altezza?*"

A blink, and a turning of the frown upside down.

"*Ah! La bella Madama Morlanda! E Milord Bennetto! Bentornati a Napoli. Benvenuti a tutti. Entrate, sedetevi, tutti. Sua Altezza verrà all'istante.*"

Leaving the coachman in charge of our baggage, we shuffled inside, being shown this time straight up to the *piano nobile* and offered seats in the *salone*. In this case, an instant was a much shorter time than when we had pitched up on Filippo's doorstep after our brush with the pirates on the way to Corfu. [19] The prince arrived when we had scarce arranged our seats.

"Milord Bennet, Milady Bennet!" he cried, embracing us both rather enthusiastically, with

[19] See *Our Neighbour's Sport beyond the Seas.*

kisses on both cheeks. "And the good Dottore Morlando and his beautiful and so charming lady. Benvenuti alla mia casa, benvenuti a tutti. But I see you have brought new friends with you. May I have the honour of knowing who these elegant newcomers are?"

"This is my eldest daughter, Jane," I replied, and her husband, Signor Bingley, lord of the manor of Garthdale, in Yorkshire."

"Ah! So! Sono diletto di conoscervi, Milord Beenglee, Milady Beenglee. Vi abbraccio."

Now it was Jane and Bingley's turn to turn red under an unaccustomed embrace.

Bingley merely mumbled and turned redder, but Jane at least managed an embarrassed *"Mi scusi, signor, non parlo Italiano."*

"We are sorry to arrive like this, without warning, and with so little in the way of boxes and such, but there is a story behind it. For now, may we impose upon you until the next steamer for Marseilles departs?"

"But then I shall only have you for a week, for the last one left only yesterday. No matter, we shall do what we can. Your old rooms are preparing as we speak, with Madama Caterina's for our new friends, and hot baths in all of them, for you look, if you will forgive me for saying so, as if you have come from some hard travelling on our execrable Italian roads."

"It is too good of you, your highness."

"Not at all, not at all. It is good for an old man to have visitors, and I see so few people nowadays, now that the Gesualdi and the Sanseveri are gone from the city, and the Borbonesi are everywhere. You will be doing me a service, entertaining me just as much as I entertain you. I only regret you cannot stay longer, and allow me to show you the sights of the Queen of Cities. Milord and Milady Beenlee must *Vedere Napoli* before they leave. The *poi morire* bit is not immediately compulsory, you know. But you must tell me your story, later. Do not concern yourselves about dress, I beg, for I can see that you have lost most of your gear. I shall have gowns sent up to you, and we shall have a quiet little supper among friends when the heat of the day is over, and you may tell me your story then."

After what we had been through, the week we spent in Naples seemed almost idyllic, or so Jane told me afterwards, while rhapsodising on the charms of Vesuvius, of Santa Lucia, of Pozzuoli, of Capodimonte and many other delights.

Morland and Margaret saw little of these sights, and I saw nothing at all, for my fever returned during our first night in the palazzo, as Morland had warned me it might, and I was not myself until the evening before the *Re Carlo* was due to arrive from Civitavecchia, before returning to Marseilles via Civitavecchia, Leghorn, and Genoa.

We had remedied much of our shortage of baggage by the time we left, the cordwainers of Naples having benefitted almost as much as the tailors, milliners, and dressmakers in the absence of my restraining hand.

The prince escorted us to the docks and saw us installed on board the steamer.

"Goodbye, old friend," he said as we embraced before crossing the gangplank. "I do not think we shall see each other again. Give my regards to Carlo Eppurt, and tell him I still think sometimes, of the days we used to torment Bonaparte's soldiers."

He was still standing there when we cast off and steamed out into the bay, waving until he was no more to be seen.

"Come," said Jane, taking my arm and leading me below. "You are still very shaky, you know. Best have a lie down. Or are you waiting for him to sing *Soave sia il vento?*"

"No," I answered. "But we would all wish for a *benigno respondo ai nuostri desir*, would we not?"

And a *benigno ritorno* for your travel-weary father,

F. Bennet.

Chapter Forty-four : Mr Bennet to Mrs Darcy - Civitavecchia.

Civitavecchia   4
June 1837

Dear Lizzie,

I have prided myself on being relatively immune to *mal de mer* in the Mediterranean, but pride cometh before a fall, and I spent most of the first leg of our voyage in my bunk. It was exhaustion, I am sure, both nervous and physical after our adventurous journey and our abrupt flight from Rome, which, looking back, I concede was probably both needless and pointless. However, at our first port of call, something happened which acted far better to restore me than all Morland's Jesuit's Bark tea and tinctures of Wormwood and of Opium.

We had debated quite vigorously during the voyage from Naples as to what we should do during the two days that the vessel stopped at Civitavecchia. The ladies were all for sending one of the gentlemen to Rome, to bring back Arianna and our trunks and boxes.

"After all," said Jane, "It is only Papa that the authorities arrested. He needs to stay on the ship; I quite agree with that, but Charles or James should not meet with any trouble."

"I was not present at the meeting," I retorted, "but may I remind you precisely who it was who took Pennworth's letter to the Cardinal and enlisted his aid for my deliverance from the Inquisitor? It was Bingley and the Doctor, was it not? And did they not afterwards abscond secretly from Rome with me? Did we not all depart surreptitiously? Will we not all now be on the *Index*

Expurgatorius, or whatever it is the Roman Church now calls the list of those wanted for questioning?"

"I take your point, Mr Bennet," replied Bingley, "But it is so inconvenient to be without one's luggage. Your friend the Neapolitan prince has been very generous in fitting us out the way he has, but, even so, it is very inconvenient. Surely I could hire a horse and ride to Rome and bring Arianna and our clothes and possessions back with me? Or, better yet, hire a carriage of some sort and load everything into it for the return journey. No-one will take any notice of me, I am sure. No-one ever has yet, apart from Jane and Darcy, and I cannot believe I am now an object of interest to the Papal police."

"That is because you have never spent any time in what is called a police state," I replied. "The rest of us have quite vivid recollections of being followed everywhere by police spies in Venice. The Romans may not be as efficient as the Austrians, but I dare say they will have a copy of this ship's passenger list before anyone may disembark."

"Oh! Mr Bennet, Mr Bennet!" cried Mrs Bennet, "Do you mean to tell me they will know we are here? Will they not pursue us and take us into custody?"

"They cannot, my dear, as long as we remain on board. While we stay on this ship, we are not in the Papal States, but in the Kingdom of the Two Sicilies. To remove us forcibly from Sicilian soil would be to risk war with Naples, and Filippo Catapani may despise the Bourbon court, but he has enough influence there to make much of such an outrage. We are safe while we stay on this vessel, but once we set foot on Papal soil we risk arrest."

"Then, by all means, let us stay on board," insisted Jane, "it will be but for a few more days, and I truly never thought much of Charles' idea of a mad dash to Rome and back."

Thus matters had stood when we departed to our bunks, but when daylight found us tied up along the quayside at Civitavecchia, from the window of the deckhouse, I could see Bingley edging towards the gangway, as if hankering to put his plan into action.

He might well have done just that, had not the sight of two of the passengers waiting to embark changed his mind, and brought him dashing back to the saloon where the rest of us were still breakfasting.

"Good news!" he cried. "So good that you will not credit it!"

The precise nature of that good news I will leave the bearers of it to explain, but I leave you in the sure and certain knowledge that it will be quite as gratifying to you as ever it was to

Your deplorably mysterious father

F. Bennet

Chapter Forty-five : News at Last – Mr Bennet to Mrs Darcy

Marseilles

10 May 1837

Dear Lizzie,

This letter may well be a surprise to you. Let me celebrate this beautiful morning by putting your mind at rest.

First of all, we are safe and sound, and rejoicing to be out of the range of any interest either the Holy Office or the Cardinal may have in us.

Second, we have secured passage on a coastal craft leaving tomorrow at some unearthly time in the morning. Why do mariners always insist on such uncomfortable departure times? Morland tells me they try to secure an outgoing tide to assist them in their departure, but I think they only do it to annoy. He cannot be right about the tide, for one thing, as there are no tides in the Mediterranean.

We plan to come back as comfortably as may be. We have a particular reason for doing so, which shall be explained in due course. Our coaster will take us as far as Cette, whence there are good roads by way of Narbonne and Toulouse which will take us to Bordeaux, where we are assured of regular sailings to England.

You may object that this route will take us across the dreaded Bay of Biscay-Oh. If you do, please do not tell your mother. She has only consented to the long sea passage because she has something else to occupy her mind just now. Precisely what that is I will leave for someone else to tell you, but your mother is certainly well pleased by it, as are we all, and I hope you will be.

Besides, Bordeaux is not really Biscay.

I have been mysterious for quite long enough now, so I will end with a recommendation that you read the enclosures herewith, which I made sure had already been sent you from Genoa, if not Civitavecchia itself, but find myself mistaken. If you read them in the order you come to them, my hope is that they will make you feel quite as superior as

Your ludicrously smug father,

F. Bennet

Chapter Forty-six : Mr Frank Darcy to Mrs Darcy – A Plea in Mitigation

~~Genoa~~ Marseilles
~~4 June~~ 1837
10 June

Dear Mama,

Grandfather tells us that you have been worried because you have not heard from us for some time.

It is very silly of you to worry, you know. We are both perfectly capable of taking care of ourselves, and I, for one, am particularly devoted to taking care of my darling Mina.

We are both truly sorry that you had so long to wait for news. It is entirely our fault for being both thoughtless and dilatory. We dawdled along our route so much that Grandpapa and his party arrived in Italy before we did.

Even then, we took our time. We tarried in Turin, we meandered in Milan, we relaxed in Ravenna.

Ravenna! There is a place that would be like heaven to Grandpapa. The Duomo at Milan, and other places like Sant Ambrogio where Mina made some sketches of Stilicho's tomb which we hope will please Grandpapa were impressive enough. But, Ravenna! Words fail me to describe San Vitale, and it is but one of the many wonders that tiny city affords the tourist. I have never seen such mosaics as are scattered about the city and its environs in my whole life. Those at Torcello, where grandpapa took me when we were in Venice are but a pale shadow by comparison. I can only hope that Mina's watercolour of the panel at San Vitale with Justinian stamping on Belisarius's foot will provide some consolation.

It was not until we arrived in Florence that we had any inkling that we were sought after. The inn keeper there said that they had had an English guest some time ago who had enquired about a Mr Darcy. He could not remember the name of this Englishman, but was certain it was not Darcy, which was a relief, I may assure you. The thought of Papa leaving his Westminster bench and pursuing us across Italy was not a happy one. He recalled that this particular Englishman was an old man, in ill health, and had a large party, including his physician, attending him, so we concluded that he must be some rich invalid taking the tour. That it might be grandpapa never occurred to me, for I have never thought of him as an old man.

It was only when we reached Rome and went to the *Albergo del Tonno* as cousin Pennworth recommended that I learned the name of the 'crazy Englishman' who had been asking for Mr Darcy. I also learned that he had left town under mysterious circumstances, and was being sought by the police.

This was definitely something I had not expected, but there could be no doubt from the landlord's description of the '*pazzo Vecchio Inglese con sua figlia molto bella e il suo proprio medico Famoso,*' of the identity of those seeking us.

The landlord was a mine of information. He told us all about the goings on of this infamous party, how Signora Bennetto had fallen prey to a so-called Count, notorious for battening upon

English ladies of a certain age, and spent most of the evenings and late into the night at parties with him; how her husband did not resent this in the customary way, but spent his time chasing after the beautiful wife of the medico; how the same Signor Bennetto had taken up with all sorts of disreputable bad lots and smugglers, and often brought back bundles of loot from his daily assignations with them.

Having thus had an entire new side of a scholar's life revealed to us, Mina and I sat down to debate what we should do next. We were both resolved to follow after our family, having become just a little sated with the wonders of Italy, and being faced with such a plethora of choice in Rome as almost to make choice impossible. But which way to turn in our search? And how should we catch up with them? Judging by the landlord's information they had at least a month's start on us.

We decided, at last, to set out for Naples, where Grandpapa has friends, in the hope that he would have done so too. At least we might hear any news of the fugitives from Prince Catapani, and at worst we would have a chance of proving the old saw wrong, by seeing Naples and living to return homewards on the next steamer.

This plan, however, was brought to nought by the events of the following day, which I will leave my darling wife to relate to you, only stipulating that although the news may please you, it cannot please you half as much as

Your proud and delighted son,

Frank Darcy

Chapter Forty-seven: Mrs Frank Darcy to Mrs Darcy

~~Genoa~~ Marseilles
~~4 June~~ 1837
10 June

Dear Mrs Darcy,

Please excuse my husband for his lack of both sensitivity and literary ability. I am still at the stage where the amazing fact that he is my husband far outweighs everything else, but even I can see that we have been neglectful.

There is no excuse for our default. We had many other things on our minds, and the days never seemed quite long enough, but we should still have made time to keep you informed. We were continually on the point of doing so, but, somehow, something else always came along to distract us.

The latest distraction was when we arrived at Civitavecchia in time to book passages on the Marseilles boat, and saw the entire family, almost, lined up on deck to greet us.

The Prince of Serendip could not have been more delighted than these two parties who had spent the whole winter and into the spring chasing each other around Italy.

We should have spent the entire time while the ship was in port exclaiming and reminiscing, had not Mr Bennet, with his usual acuity, explained the situation in which our elders found themselves, and, while carefully not framing a direct request, pointed out how welcome would be an opportunity to recover their servant and their baggage, both of which had been abandoned in Rome for reasons which were 'a long story', to be related thereafter.

Dear Frank instantly volunteered himself for the task.

"I cannot quite believe in the Spanish Inquisition," he said, "but I can believe that I may ride to Rome and back in a day, and it will be useful to have something that I may point out to Mama as a good deed done.

There will be no danger. The police are looking for an elderly English gentleman called Bennet. They have no reason to associate him with a young English gentleman called Darcy, but newly arrived in Rome, and known for dashing about in his curricle at all sorts of inconvenient hours. As for the direction, we must have walked past that place a dozen times while we were in Rome. I shall go directly there and come directly back, and all manner of things shall be well."

And off he went, bless him, leaving me to experience a different form of distraction, for every minute he was gone I could think of nothing else, and I swear everyone must have thought me quite gone in my wits until the return of my Ulysse.

Distraction is no more than an excuse, and a very feeble one, I know, but I sincerely hope that one of the things that turned out well will, at least, serve as some consolation. You must have been very anxious to hear our news, and I shudder to think what may have passed through your mind when you heard nothing.

I rather believe that I have the right to be able to lay claim to understanding the feelings of a mother, or, at any rate, I soon will. We were already on our way back to England when we found Mr Bennet and his party, and hope to be home in good time for the lying in.

If it is a girl, we are both agreed that we shall call her Elizabeth. We have not yet been able to agree upon a boy's name, although you may guess that there has been no shortage of suggestions.

Feel free to add your own suggestion as you see fit.

We hope to be back at Pemberley by the end of the month.

Until then, please excuse

Your dilatory, devoted, delighted daughter,

Mina.

Chapter Forty-eight – Mrs Darcy to Mrs Darcy- Mixed News

Pemberley

22 June 1837

My very dear Mina,

What a joy it was to read your letter! Such good news, just when we were in need of good news.

You will not have heard as yet, but Mr Darcy arrived late last night, fresh from Westminster with the latest.

The King died two days ago, and all the nation is in mourning. *De mortuis non nisi bonum*, as my father would say, so there really is not much more to relate. Your father-in-law says there will have to be a fresh election, and he has not decided yet whether he will stand again.

There will be the state funeral, of course, and then the coronation. How a seventeen-year-old slip of a girl will manage the responsibilities she must inherit, who can tell?

I am determined not to let this put a damper on your news, however, and while I must now say 'the King is dead, God save the Queen' I will also offer up prayers for the future master of Pemberley, and his darling parents.

Come back to us quickly, all of you, and delight the heart of

Your doting mother-in-law,

Elizabeth Darcy.

THE END

Other Books by Ronald McGowan

Jane Austen Amplifications

> Pride Unprejudiced
>
> To Make Sport for our Neighbours
>
> More Sport for our Neighbours
>
> Our Neighbours' Sport Beyond the Seas
>
> Naples to Northanger
>
> Colonel Brandon's Secret
>
> Miss Margaret's Mission
>
> Mansfield Restored
>
> The Journal of Miss Jane Fairfax
>
> Miss Darcy's Diversions
>
> Perception and Persuasion
>
> Miss Bingley's Banishment

Novels of Miss Margaret Dashwood

> The Seven Sisters, or Arrogance and Attitude
>
> Southover Priory

The Golden Apple Series

The Judgment of Paris

The Wrath of Achilles

The Return of the Achaeans

Other Books

What I did in my Holidays

Barset Revisited

Read them all on Kindle or in hard copies available via Amazon or your local bookshop.